ALPHA PAN

Terra-form 1

Becca Van

MENAGE EVERLASTING

Siren Publishing, Inc.
www.SirenPublishing.com

A SIREN PUBLISHING BOOK
IMPRINT: Ménage Everlasting

ALPHA PANTHERS
Copyright © 2012 by Becca Van

ISBN-10: 1-61926-933-3
ISBN-13: 978-1-61926-933-0

First Printing: April 2012

Cover design by Les Byerley
All art and logo copyright © 2012 by Siren Publishing, Inc.

Printed in the U.S.A.

PUBLISHER
Siren Publishing, Inc.
www.SirenPublishing.com

DEDICATION

This book is dedicated to all the people who read my books.
Thanks so much for your support.

ALPHA PANTHERS

Terra-form 1

BECCA VAN
Copyright © 2012

Chapter One

April Waterson waved good-bye to her friend and work colleague, Olivia Hammond, after a night out for dinner and a few drinks at the end of a long, tiring week at work. April had always had trust issues from as far back as early childhood, and the fact that she and Olivia were so close was often a pleasant surprise to her. April had learned to cover up her insecurities with her tongue and hostility because of her parents. She was too wary to let her guard down and accept people and situations at face value.

April headed down the small, dimly lit, enclosed walkway toward the cabstand behind the club. She glanced around nervously. The quiet on the street was unnatural, and she realized she was quite alone, late at night. The unreality of the quiet seeped into her body and mind, making her heartbeat pick up and her breathing escalate. She couldn't even hear any traffic noises. Something wasn't right, but she couldn't work out what.

April was no more than twenty yards from the cabstand when a strange, light-headed sensation assailed her. She felt as if she was walking through quicksand, her body moving in slow motion, her limbs feeling very heavy, as she kept her eyes on the end of the walkway. Dizziness began to make her feel woozy, and black spots formed before her eyes. April berated herself for the third glass of wine she had before she left the club. She never really did have a head for alcohol. One glass was enough to get her tipsy even with a belly full of food.

The dizziness increased with every step she took. Her body felt as if it were detached from her brain, but she knew she was still moving. The dark spots before her eyes increased until she felt totally blind. Her lips were open, and air was panting in and out of her lungs rapidly, as if she had been running for a long time. Blood was roaring through her ears until she could hear nothing else. April knew she was in trouble and tried to call out, but her body would not cooperate. She felt disconnected from her physical self, as if she were floating outside of herself. Her body was a total dead weight, out of her control. Just as she thought she was going to pass out, her eyes began to adjust, the darkness slowly receding. Her breathing slowed, and the roaring in her ears diminished. She blinked a few times and slowly turned in a circle.

What the fuck? Where the hell am I?

April was surrounded by trees. All around her were giant trees, their green foliage-covered limbs reaching to the sky. It was still night time, and April wondered if someone had somehow slipped something into her drink. She had to be hallucinating. That would explain the dizziness she had experienced and also the fact she had somehow landed in a forest.

April gave a whimper of fear, still not sure what was going on but too scared to move in case she was hallucinating. The last thing she wanted to do was end up in the middle of a busy road without realizing it. She slowly lowered herself to the ground, leaning against the massive trunk of a tree. The bark on her bare shoulders felt real enough. Maybe she was leaning on a tree on the side of the road. Too scared to move, she stayed where she was, hoping someone would find her and help her or that the drug she had hypothetically been given would wear off. She thanked God she'd had the foresight to change into jeans before leaving the office. They were a lot warmer than the skirt she'd had on. She pulled a black cardigan she'd also placed in her large purse out and slid her arms through the sleeves to cover the red halter top she was wearing. She hated being cold and always made sure to carry some sort of extra covering in case she needed it.

April got a little more comfortable on the soft bed of leaves then laid her head back against the trunk of the tree. She could hear animals rustling around in the undergrowth of the forest and hoped like hell that, wherever she was, she wouldn't end up being a wild animal's dinner. She was so tired she was having trouble keeping her eyelids from sliding closed. She caught herself drifting into sleep then jerked awake as her head nodded forward. She needed to keep alert and not let the drugs affect her by sending her to sleep. She was afraid she wouldn't wake up again. That was her last thought as her eyes slid closed for the last time, her breathing even and deep as she lost her fight against exhaustion.

* * * *

Gage smelled the human female and knew she was miles away from their present location. He nudged his brother, another large black panther, in the shoulder and tilted his head as he sniffed the air. He saw his brother sniff the air and heard his low growl. He copied his brother, growling low in his throat as the delectable scent of the female wafted on the breeze. Gage looked at his brother and, with silent communication, abandoned the prey they had been stalking and took off. The feel of his muscles rippling as he sped through the forest to get to their quarry was exhilarating. He loved the feel of the wind running through his fur, like the tips of fingers caressing and massaging his body lightly. He felt so free and alive, but he was also determined. He wanted, needed, to get to the female before any of the other shifter kind knew of her presence in the forest. He and his brother had been searching for a female for so long they had just about given up hope of finding a mate of their own. He knew as soon as he had smelled her scent, she was their mate. Nothing and no one was going to get in their way of claiming their woman. Not even their mate, herself.

Gage and Saxon Kian stood yards away from the sleeping human female. Gage studied her body as he inhaled her delectable scent. The musky aroma of her pussy pulled at his heart and cock, making his cock throb with unrequited desire and his heart fill as the emptiness within receded. Their mate was small compared to him and Saxon. He could tell by the length of her shapely legs, encased in some sort of heavy black material. She had long blonde hair and a sleek but curvy body. He wanted to change forms, pick up his mate, and take her back to their lair, but he knew they were going to have to mark her, claim her, before any of the other shape-shifters living in their vicinity could scent their woman.

Gage was the elder of the two by no more than five minutes, but they were both Alpha males and generally made any decisions together. This time, however, Gage silently communicated his demand to claim the female to his brother, not willing to back down an inch. The two brothers were able to communicate telepathically, and he was thankful for that ability right now. The last thing he wanted to do was scare their mate away.

Gage and Saxon slowly crept in toward the female, keeping their bodies low to the ground as they stalked their prey. The closer they got to the female, the more his muscles and cock hardened with desire. The scent of her skin was a delicious mix of vanilla, honey, and female musk, which called to his beast's primitive urges. He knew his brother would want what he wanted, to cover their mate's body with their own and fuck her into oblivion. When he and Saxon were standing on either side of their mate, they carefully leaned forward, their noses close to the skin on her neck and shoulder. They kept their eyes on their mate as Gage communicated with his brother.

We mark her on the count of three, Sax. Are you ready? Gage asked his brother telepathically.

Yes. Are you sure we should mark her first? What if she doesn't like us? Saxon was always more sensitive than Gage. He was able to place himself in other people's situations more readily than Gage. Gage had a more dominant personality than his brother. When he made a decision, he acted on that decision, without wavering, and dealt with the consequences as they cropped up. Saxon was also a dominant male, but he thought things through thoroughly before he acted.

We'll work on that after we claim her. Do you want to give any of the other shifters around here a chance to claim our mate? You know as well as I do, she could be a mate to some of the other kind, Gage replied.

The last thing either of them wanted was for another species of shifters to find and mark their mate. Saxon acquiesced to his brother. *Okay, I'm ready.*

All right, on three, and don't bite down too hard or too deep. We don't want to hurt our mate too much. One, two, three.

* * * *

April woke up screaming. She felt something bite into her skin where her shoulders met her neck. She screamed at the top of her lungs and then whimpered in fear as she stared into the golden eyes of two of the largest panthers she had ever seen. She was totally terrified and knew she was a goner. She was going to end up dinner for wild beasts, after all. Her body was shaking so much she could feel her teeth chattering. She was so scared she was in danger of peeing her pants. The heads of the two muscle-packed panthers were nearly as big as her whole torso. She prayed to God she wouldn't feel too much pain as they killed her. That was her last thought, as fear consumed her, causing her to faint.

* * * *

April woke with a start. She jerked upright and found herself alone in a massive timber bed in a brightly lit room. The room was so large her apartment could have fit into it five times over. The floor was made of marble, and the furnishings scattered around were luxurious. She was in what looked like a palace with lavish furnishings. There were timber chests of drawers, as well as navy-blue velvet material hanging down from the bed posts, creating a deceptive feeling of privacy. The last thing she remembered was staring into the golden, glowing eyes of two massive black panthers. She knew she must have been hallucinating, but she still had no idea where she was.

April stretched and yawned, then gasped with horror as she realized she was totally naked. She hoped whoever had relieved her of her clothes was female. There was nothing she could do about it now. She had no idea where she was or who had rescued her from the massive black panthers intending to eat her for their dinner, but she was too thankful she was alive to worry about where she really was. She flung the covers back, stood, and walked across the cold marble floor to the door on the opposite side of the room.

April gasped with awe as she opened the door to a massively proportioned bathroom. The walls and floor were a light marble color with streaks of gray, pink, and gold running through it. The sunken bathtub was large enough for ten people or more, and was full of steaming water. The shower on the other side of the room was encased in large glass panels, with many gold water spigots jutting out of the walls.

April slid into the fragrant pool of water then swam over to the opposite end beneath the water. She came up, took a deep breath, and, to her delight, found contoured bench seats. She made herself comfortable then picked up one of the many bottles of fragrant bath gel and sniffed. She went through the sniffing process several times, until she found a scent to her liking. It was similar to the vanilla-and-honey gel she used at home. Once she was feeling clean and refreshed, she got out of the pool, dried off, then rummaged around under the cupboards beneath the three marble sinks, looking for a toothbrush and paste. She found what she was looking for and, when done, walked back out of the bathroom, a large, fluffy towel wrapping her body. She froze in her tracks when she saw two of the tallest, sexiest, most masculine men she had ever seen in her life.

They both had to be at least seven feet tall, if not taller. They had shoulder-length black hair, massively wide shoulders, huge biceps and pectoral muscles, which tapered down over ripped abs, slim hips, and long, muscular legs. Neither man had a shirt on, and their legs were covered in what looked like black-leather, formfitting pants. The pants were so tight they left nothing to April's imagination, and she could see they both had the largest erections she had ever seen. While she knew her experience was limited, she had seen pictures of aroused naked men before, and she knew they were huge. A female instinctively knew this sort of thing. April gave a start, and she felt heat creep up her cheeks with embarrassment when she realized where she was staring. She moved her eyes back up to their faces, and her breath caught in her throat.

The two men were twins. They were Adonises personified. They had firm, square jaws and grooves running adjacent to their full, sensual lips, which she knew would turn into dimples when they smiled. Their cheekbones were sharp, and their eyes were the lightest green she had ever seen. Their eyes had a slight slant to them, reminding her of the eyes of a feline. April was quite tall for a female at five foot nine, but standing near these two giants, she felt small and feminine for the first time in her life. She noticed they were perusing her features and body just as she had done theirs. She began to feel uncomfortable when they continued to look at her without speaking, hunger and heat evident in their eyes. April cleared her throat and hoped she wouldn't sound like a mouse, squeaking out her first words to the two sexy men.

"Who are you, and where am I?"

"I am Gage Kian, and this is my brother, Saxon. You are in our home. We found you in the forest all alone and thought it would be best to bring you here, where we knew you would be safe."

"Where is here? Where is your home, and where are my clothes?"

"We are in Terra-form. Where did you think you were? What is your name?" Gage asked.

April tried to cover up the shiver working its way up her spine. Gage's deep, raspy voice sent goose bumps of pleasure over her body.

"April. I'm April Waterson. Where the hell is Terra-form? I've never heard of it before."

"How did you get here, April?" Saxon asked.

The sound of his voice was different than his brother's. His voice made her think of smooth silk caressing over her body, as his deep cadence was a lot less rough than his brother's.

"I don't know," April replied quietly. "One moment I was walking to a cabstand, the next I felt dizzy, totally disorientated, like I was trying to walk through quicksand. My vision went, and when it came back, I was in a forest surrounded by massive trees."

Gage looked to Saxon with a raised eyebrow. It looked to April as if they were communicating silently, but that just wasn't possible. She hadn't heard either of them speak a word.

"What is a cabstand?" Saxon asked, turning his gaze back on her as she shifted on her feet nervously. She thought she saw Saxon's eyes turn a gold color and then back to green. She blinked and gave a mental shrug, thinking she must have imagined it. He was eying her as if he wanted to rip the towel from her body, place her on the bed, and mount her. She shifted again and saw Gage was staring at her the same way.

"You don't know what a cabstand is?" April asked, her voice escalating as her panic began to surface. She watched as first Saxon then Gage shook their heads in negation. "What about a car?" Once again, they looked at her and shook their heads.

"What year is it?" April asked with trepidation.

"It is 2011. Where is your home, April?" asked Gage.

"Lincoln, Nebraska, United States of America, planet Earth," April replied with a quaver in her voice and lifted her chin to the two men, staring at them arrogantly as if daring them to refute her statement. She was all of a sudden very afraid, not sure if she was even on Earth anymore. Maybe she had been beamed up to another planet. Her heartbeat picked up speed, thumping rapidly against her breasts.

"Yes, planet Earth, Terra-form. What is United States of America?" Saxon asked with a frown.

"Oh my God. Oh my God. Oh my God," April chanted as she stared at the two large men. She stumbled on wobbly legs over to the large bed and sat on the side of it, afraid her legs would give out beneath her. She had no idea how she had gotten here, but she knew she was no longer on Earth as she knew it. Yet the brothers had told her it was indeed the year 2011.

What the hell has happened? What have I stumbled into?

The only thought she could come up with was an alternate reality plane to planet Earth. And if that was the case, how in the hell was she supposed to get back home?

* * * *

Gage watched their sexy mate stumble over to the large bed. He listened to her chant and watched as she sat on the side of the bed. The color had drained from her face, leaving her skin looking translucent in the brightly lit room. Her small body was covered by a large, white, fluffy towel, and her damp hair hung down to the middle of her back in disarray. She was a beautiful female. Her eyes were sky blue, her skin a creamy white, and she had curves in all the right places. Gage remembered what their mate looked like naked and wanted to rip the towel from her body, spread her legs, and lap at the cream between her thighs until he'd had his fill of her delectable juices. Then he wanted to fuck until neither of them could walk. He growled low in his throat, his hard cock pulsing in his tight pants. He began to purr as he imagined lapping at his mate's cunt to his heart's content. A punch to his arm from Saxon brought him out of his daydream. His eyes connected with his mate's. She was looking at him as if he had lost his mind.

"What are you?" April asked, moving up onto the bed, hunching against the headboard, as far away from him and Saxon as possible.

Gage couldn't seem to find his tongue as he stood staring at his mate. He could feel his beast pushing against him, trying to take over so the mating could begin. Gage was having a hell of a time trying to control his beast. He turned away from April as he tried to regain control.

"I will get you something to wear. Sunup meal is almost ready," Gage said over his shoulder, and then he left the room. He shifted to his beast as soon as he was out of sight and ran through the palace halls. Hopefully releasing his beast and running off some pent-up energy would be enough to soothe his animal for a time.

* * * *

"April, please do not be afraid of us. We would never do anything to hurt you," Saxon said, moving closer to his mate. The scent of fear, adrenaline, and arousal was rolling off of her in waves. Saxon knew they needed to keep their mate as calm as possible. Otherwise she would end up fighting them every step of the way. The last thing he wanted was for his and his brother's beasts to take over and scare their mate. Saxon had never seen Gage lose control of his beast before. He was always in control and usually the one to pull Saxon up. But then, neither of them had ever been near their mate before. Saxon just hoped that once they told April what they were, she didn't run away from them screaming in fear.

Chapter Two

April watched as Saxon approached the bed. She didn't move away from him, but felt her muscles bunch up, ready to take flight. She exhaled as Saxon sat down on the end of the bed and turned toward her. She could see the concern for her in his eyes and slowly released the tension from her taut muscles.

"I don't know how you came to be here, April, but I am glad you are here. We have been searching for you for such a long time. We had almost given up hope of ever finding you," Saxon stated.

"What…what do you mean you've been searching for me? You don't even know me."

"You are our mate, April. We never thought we would find you. You are the other half of us."

"What? What do you mean your mate? What are you? Where the hell am I? I want to go home!" April yelled the last statement, tears tracking down her cheeks.

April didn't see him move. One moment Saxon was at the end of the bed, the next he was pulling her into his arms and onto his lap. He crooned to her in his deep, melodious voice as she cried against his large, warm, muscular chest. She clung to him as the last several hours finally caught up with her. She was alone and scared in a strange place, with no idea how she had gotten here, and no way to get back home. Her tears finally slowed and dried as she lay curled up on Saxon's lap. She felt so small, safe, and feminine. She had never felt like that before. She was so used to looking at a man from the same eye level and knew her height often intimidated some males. She'd only ever had one true boyfriend, and that had turned out to be a total disaster, because he had taken her out, wined and dined her, and had eventually fucked her on a bet. It seemed some of her work colleagues had gotten it into their minds that because she was so tall, she must have balls. When her ex had finally gotten into her pants and taken her virginity, he'd left her with a smirk, advising her he would let his friends know she was indeed a woman after all. April had vowed then and there she would never, ever have another relationship with a man.

April had always felt so awkward around other men and women. She was actually quite a clumsy person, and the only person she had ever really connected with was Olivia. She had met Olivia three years ago when April had applied for and gotten the job of secretary in a small publishing company. April and Olivia had been fast friends ever since. The two young women had hit it off from the first and made it a habit to unwind at the end of each week with dinner and drinks.

Olivia was everything a man looked for in a woman. She was small in stature and frame, as well as curvy in all the right places. April felt like an Amazon when she was standing with the shorter, more feminine woman and always seemed to be overlooked by males when she was with her friend. They tended to see her as a buddy, rather than a woman with the same urges and feelings as every other female.

Olivia had no idea how beautiful and feminine she was, and she didn't seem to notice the male attention she received. It was like she was totally oblivious to the male species. April knew her friend wasn't homosexual, but she had an idea why Olivia kept men at arm's length. She knew one day her friend would confide in her once she was ready, so April didn't push Olivia with questions. They were two peas in a pod. They were both wary of men. Neither of them was willing to give an inch when approached by the opposite sex. In the time they had been friends, neither she nor Olivia had been on a date. Except for now, it seemed.

April did something totally uncharacteristic to her and snuggled her face into Saxon's warm chest, closing her eyes as she breathed in his clean, masculine scent. His scent drew her to him, like a moth to a flame, and she wanted nothing more than to slide her hands up and down that delectable, rock-hard male body. April felt the change in Saxon's breathing, and his cock hardened beneath her butt. She wanted to rip her towel off, as well as his tight pants, and impale herself on his hard rod. A deep ache began in her pussy, making her internal muscles clench and release. She could feel juices gathering into a pool in her vagina then seeping out to dampen her thighs, and she hoped like hell Saxon couldn't smell her arousal. Even though her body was telling her for the first time in years that she wanted a male, her head was telling her to back off, and fast. April sat up and pushed away from Saxon. She moved quickly to the other side of the room, as far away from the tempting male as she was able to get. She was panting heavily and knew her cheeks were flushed as she stared at the sexy man still sitting on the bed. When her breathing finally evened out and she felt she was once more in control, she went back to questioning Saxon.

"What are you, Saxon?"

"We are shape-shifters, April. Our forest is full of different *were* kind. We are of the panther clan, but there are others, such as bears, coyotes, wolves, lions, tigers, and a few others I cannot remember right now."

"It was you, wasn't it? You and your brother bit me last night. What the hell did you do that for? You scared the shit out of me. I thought you were going to eat me for dinner. How the hell is this even possible? Please, I don't belong here. You need to help me get home."

"Enough, April." Gage's deep, raspy voice penetrated April's frantic mind. She turned her head to see him closing the bedroom door behind him and moving further into the room. "You are becoming hysterical. You are our mate. We have already claimed you. There is no way we are letting you go home now. You are going to have to come to terms with that."

"You've claimed me? What the fuck gave you the right to claim me, like I was some sort of possession? I can't believe this shit. Where are my clothes?" April yelled.

* * * *

Gage had had enough. He knew April was ranting and screaming because she was afraid, but he wasn't going to let her get away with disrespecting him. He slowly walked toward her and saw her eyes widen with apprehension, and she nodded at him in quiet acquiescence. He didn't stop, just kept right on going until April had backed herself into the wall. He had her totally at his mercy. He stopped when he could feel the heat emanating from her delicious little body. She was so small and fragile compared to his great size. He breathed in the sweet scent of her female musk, but he could also smell her underlying fear. He didn't want to scare his little mate, but he couldn't hold himself back anymore. He wanted to taste her sweet, luscious mouth, and he had every intention of doing so.

Gage heard April whimper as he moved his hands down to her small waist. He gripped her in his hands, being careful not to squeeze her too hard, and lifted her up until she was eye level with him. He stared deeply into her sky-blue eyes and felt himself drowning within their depths. He slowly lowered his head closer to hers, until his lips were resting on hers lightly, a butterfly of a touch. He could feel her hot, sweet, moist breath panting out onto his lips and moved that last fraction of an inch, taking her mouth with a ravenous hunger. He slanted his mouth over hers, parting her lips with his own, making room to thrust his tongue into the depths of her sweet mouth. He growled low in approval at the first taste of her sweetness and knew he would never be able to get enough of his mate.

Gage moved one of his massive arms, until the palm of his hand was beneath the cheeks of April's ass, supporting her slight weight as he kissed her hungrily. He began to purr deep in his throat as his mate tentatively slid her tongue along the length of his. Her slight, hesitant capitulation had Gage's beast breaking free and taking over. He slanted his mouth over hers again and again, thrusting his tongue into her sweet recess, sliding his tongue over the roof of her mouth, along the inside of each of her cheeks, over her teeth, and then back to her tongue. He moaned again when he felt April wrap her arms around his neck and her legs around his waist. He grasped the globes of her ass in each hand and began to thrust his leather-covered, turgid erection against her warm, wet sex. Gage felt April's hard nipples rubbing against his chest and realized the towel she'd been wrapped in had fallen from her sexy little body. He moved quickly over to the bed, lowered her to the mattress, and followed her down without breaking the contact of their mouths. He felt the bed dip and knew Saxon had joined them on the bed.

Gage released April's lips, giving them both a chance to drag air into their oxygen-depleted lungs. He nibbled over her jaw, down the side of her neck until he reached her ear. He slid his tongue into her ear and had to hold her down as she bucked and writhed with pleasure. He knew he had just found an erogenous zone on his little mate. He swirled his tongue around the rim of her ear, then thrust it back into her small canal. He moved one of his hands, enveloping one of her soft breasts in his palm, and began to massage. He kneaded the soft, fleshy mound then pinched her nipple between his thumb and finger, making her cry out with pleasure.

Gage licked and nibbled his way down April's neck, over her collarbone, over her breast, until he reached the nipple between his finger and thumb. He moved his hand away then sucked her jutting, pink nipple into his mouth. He framed her little nub between his teeth. Then, using his tongue, he flicked and laved it until he had April sobbing for more. Gage opened his eyes and was just in time to see Saxon licking his way over their mate's soft, silky stomach. He moved off to the side of April's body so he could see his mate's face, as well as his brother in his peripheral vision. He saw Saxon spread

April's legs, then move between her thighs. Saxon growled just before lowering his head to their mate's pussy.

Gage watched as Saxon slid his tongue from the top of April's pussy down to her creamy, dripping hole. He could tell by the look on Saxon's face his brother liked the taste of their mate's juices sliding over his tongue, and he heard him swallow her essence down with a slurp and a gulp. Saxon repeated the process over and over again, and Gage knew his brother would never be able to get enough. He couldn't wait for his own taste of their mate. He saw Saxon slide his tongue back up through her slick folds, swirling it over the little bundle of nerves at the top of her sex. He moved one hand from her hips and slid the other over her pubic bone, holding their mate's hips still for his ministrations. He watched as his brother used a finger from his other hand and massaged it around the ring of her pussy hole, just dipping the tip into her vagina every so often, making April's desire burn hotter, brighter, until she was begging.

"Please, help me," April cried out.

Gage, who had just taken his mate's breast into his mouth again, lifted his head from her, releasing her nipple with a loud pop. He raised his eyes to hers, the sight of her nearly making him lose control. Her cheeks were flushed, her eyes glassy, and her pupils dilated. He was on the edge of control. He could feel his beast pushing at him to shift and fuck her like there was no tomorrow. He tried to push his beast back down, but his male feline counterpart was in too much of a hurry and pushed its way through with a surge of dominance.

He could feel the beginnings of the change and knew he wasn't going to be able to hold back. He could feel his skin tingling and knew his fur was about to make an entrance. His claws pushed through the tips of his fingers, and he knew his eyes were changing from green to golden. He felt his muscles and bones begin to contort, his mouth elongating slightly, his whiskers pushing their way through his skin beneath his nose. His bones cracked and popped, his fur erupting out to cover his flesh. His pants ripped from his body, and his tail pushed out from the base of his spine. He crouched along the mattress next to April and purred deep in his throat. The scent of her musky sex was so much more enhanced in his were-panther form than his human form. He watched April through narrowed eyes, seeing her confusion then comprehension. They were indeed what Saxon had told her.

* * * *

April couldn't believe what she was seeing. She watched as Gage changed from a human male to a huge, black panther in moments. The terrible sounds of his bones cracking and popping made her feel ill, and she was concerned that Gage was feeling pain. But she was so scared she couldn't move. She saw Saxon lift his head and stare at his brother. He moved away from between April's thighs, snaked an arm around her waist, and hauled her off the bed, up against his warm, hard chest.

"Don't move, April. Gage's beast has taken over and wants to mate with you. I don't want him coming near you in his panther form. He could hurt you if he tried to mount you when his beast is in control," Saxon whispered into April's ear.

April kept her eyes on Gage, not wanting to make any sudden moves and alarm the beast. Saxon kept her wrapped in his arms but didn't move when Gage leapt from the bed and stalked toward them.

April was shaking uncontrollably, wrapped in Saxon's arms. She wanted to spin around and climb up his body to get away from Gage. She kept her eyes on his golden ones as he came closer and closer to her and Saxon. A shiver wracked her whole body as Gage stuck his nose in her pussy and sniffed deeply. He chuffed in the back of his throat, making April jump slightly then bite her tongue hard to stop herself from screaming at him when his large, raspy tongue licked through the sensitive folds of her cunt.

"Don't move and try not to make any sound, baby. His beast isn't going to be satisfied until it's had its fill of you. Don't worry, I won't let him hurt you or fuck you in this form," Saxon stated quietly.

April was too scared to move as Gage licked her cunt. Her legs were shaking, and the feel of his abrasive tongue was too much for her to take. She cried out as his tongue flicked over her clit and sent her over the edge into her first climax. Her legs wobbled beneath her body at the sound of Gage purring deep in his throat as he kept his eyes glued to hers. She felt as if she was going to slump down onto the floor at Saxon's feet. She moved her hands up slowly and clutched onto Saxon's muscular forearms. He tightened his arms around her waist as she stared down at his brother. Gage didn't even look at his brother. He kept his eyes on hers as Saxon kept up a low, steady whisper in April's ear as he tried to keep her calm. It didn't seem to help, though. She couldn't stop shaking.

April felt the tip of Gage's tongue push up into her cunt and knew she wasn't going to be standing for much longer. Her legs were shaking like a bowl of Jell-O as Gage tongue-fucked her. She felt his elongated tongue push up further into her vagina, to rasp and twirl over a particularly sensitive spot inside her. She cried out again as her pussy contracted around the large muscle embedded in her body. She felt as if she was losing her mind. The sight of Gage shifted into a large, black panther licking her cunt should have made her feel revolted and turned off. Instead she could feel her juices dripping out of her as Gage lapped up her cream.

He withdrew his tongue from her channel and licked up through her folds again. He swirled his sandpaper-like tongue over her engorged, sensitive clit, and she knew she wouldn't be able to hold out much longer. She was on the edge of her own control, could feel rage building up as she stared down into the golden, glowing eyes of Gage's panther. She'd had just about more than she could stand. She glared into Gage's eyes, letting him know she wasn't going to stand for much more.

April could feel her body coiling into a tight spring, but she didn't want to let go. The feeling was too big, too much, and she fought it with everything she had. She let her fury build, intending to use it to keep her sanity. She was glaring at Gage through narrowed eyes and could have sworn he smiled at her as his tongue faltered on her sensitive clit. It didn't stop him for long, though. He used his muscular shoulders to push between her legs, widening her stance so he had better access to her pussy. He lifted his head, growled once, then began purring again as his tongue went back to lapping the cream from her cunt. April didn't stand a chance against the wild beast between her legs. He just kept right on going, and she knew he wouldn't stop until she either passed out from too much pleasure or he'd had his fill. Her body was shaking violently now as she used her internal muscles, trying to stave off a climax. Her muscles were coiling in taut and fast, like a rope being wrapped swiftly onto a large spool. Her body was winding tighter and tighter, her fury building higher and higher at her lack of control. All of a sudden the coil snapped, sending the rope spinning out of control. Her body bucked and convulsed as spasm after spasm consumed her, the feeling of her pulsing internal muscles and the gushing of her milky release making her lower abdomen ache with unfamiliarity. If it hadn't been for Saxon holding her, April knew she would have been in a puddle on the floor. Gage was purring in satisfaction as he licked up the last drops of her release. April's breath was bellowing in and out of her lungs. She watched with fury and irritation as Gage slowly emerged from his beast back into his male form.

April's anger reached its boiling point at the sight of him smiling at her with satisfaction. She wanted to vent her acrimony at the fact that she'd had no control over her own body as a *were*-animal made her climax. It didn't matter to her at that moment that she barely came up to his chest. When her body was finally back in her control, and her breathing wasn't as rapid as it had been, she intended to let him know her vexation at his treatment of her.

She stepped forward, ignoring the fact that he was totally naked, and looked up into his light-green eyes. She had no intention of going easy on him. She was going to lay down the law, and if he didn't respect her wishes, she was out of here. Other *weres* or not.

April moved her arm up to poke Gage in the chest, not caring in the least that her long fingernail was likely causing him pain.

"I can't believe you did that to me. I can't believe I enjoyed it. Do you think I like having climaxes forced on me by a shape-shifter? If you ever touch me or scare me again like that, in your animal form, I will rip your head from your shoulders and shove it up your ass. Do I make myself clear?" April spat through clenched teeth.

She had never been so humiliated in her life. She wanted to leave as soon as possible, and that's just what she intended to do. There was no way in hell she was staying in this zoo. She was going home, and no one was going to stop her.

* * * *

April eased her aching body into the large pool of warm water. She sighed as her body relaxed for the first time since Saxon had dragged Gage out of her room. She thanked God Gage had dropped her clothes on the floor, just inside the door to her room. Once they had gone, she had scooped them up and headed straight for the bathroom. She was totally horrified by the fact Gage had been able to get her off so many times with his tongue as a panther. She didn't think she was ever going to be able to forgive him, or herself for that matter. She had been as turned on as he had, and that, she just couldn't comprehend. She felt as if her life was totally out of her control, which it was. She had no idea where she was or how to get back home. She was at the mercy of shape-shifters who claimed to be her mates.

April sat up in her seat with a gasp. She remembered waking up against a tree trunk in pain from being bitten by two panthers. She knew she had fainted in fear. The next time she had woken was in the bedroom. She surged out of the pool and ran to the mirror on the wall. She saw the fading bite marks in the mirror on either side of her neck, where her neck and shoulder met. She had read plenty of paranormal romance novels and knew the bite marks were how Gage and Saxon had marked and claimed her as their mate. She was lying to herself, telling herself they were only using her for her body. She didn't really want to face the fact she now had an Earth equivalent of husbands. She wasn't ready to face anything just yet. God, she wished Olivia was here. She missed being able to talk things over with her best friend. She sighed and gave a mental shrug. Well, it didn't matter one way or the other. There was no way she was sticking around.

Chapter Three

April opened one of the double doors to the large bedroom and gave a sigh of relief when no one was in sight. The hallway was long, with numerous doors and other hallways leading off of it. She hoped like hell she didn't meet anyone as she tried to navigate her way out of this palatial mansion. Especially Gage and Saxon. The last thing she needed was for one of them to come upon her as she tried to escape. The thought of them both jumping her bones in their panther form made her shudder. She was not sure if it was in revulsion or desire. She pushed that thought to the back of her mind and headed down the long hallway.

April came upon a *T* intersection of corridors and turned right after she peeked around the corners to make sure everything was all clear. She ducked around the corner and took off at a quick jog, hoping to reach the double doors at the end of the corridor before anyone discovered she was missing. Her hand reached out to the gold handle and pushed the door open a crack. She peeked through the door and sighed with relief as she spied the great outdoors. She pushed the door open enough to be able to slide through the gap and quietly closed the door behind her.

April breathed easily and deeply for the first time since she'd found herself in this strange place. She had no idea where she was going. She only knew she had to get away from the two panther men claiming to be her mate. She ran toward the line of trees, off to the left side of the front door. She didn't dare look back. She was too afraid of being caught. She found a trail leading into the forest and decided that it was her best bet to stay as close to it as possible. That way if she couldn't find anywhere else to go, she would be able to make her way back to the massive palace.

April felt like she had been walking for hours. She was tired, hot, and terribly thirsty. She hadn't realized she would be walking through what seemed to be a tropical rain forest. She was sweating profusely as she walked through the hot, humid air. She wanted nothing more than to sit down and drink a gallon of water. April sighed and wondered if she should have stayed where she was. At least she knew the wild beasts in the palace wouldn't hurt her, as they hadn't so far. There could be other wild beasts traversing the forest, as Saxon had warned her. And God help her if she came upon any more shape-shifters. What would she do then?

April froze when she heard a rustle in the forest behind her. Her mind began conjuring up all sorts of scenarios, her death most prominent in her mind. She could see herself being ripped apart by lions, tigers, and bears. Oh my. April berated herself. She had to stop letting her imagination take control. She was an adult woman, for goodness sake, not a little kid still scared of the bogeyman.

April moved off of the trail just in time to see a great, lumbering bear meandering down the track. She couldn't believe her overactive imagination had been partially right. Her heart sped up and began to thump in her chest, her breathing escalated, and she quietly scanned the trees nearby. She just hoped that the bear couldn't climb, because that was what she was going to do. She grabbed the lowest limb of a tree, which was about chest height. She kicked her legs up and ended up clinging to the branch upside down. She used all the strength she had, which thankfully was enhanced by adrenaline, and swung one leg up and over the branch until it was behind her bent knee. She used her arms and began pulling herself upright. By the time she had her breath back, she was able to look down and nearly squealed with fright. The big, brown bear was sitting down below, watching her and sniffing the air.

April didn't stop to think. She clung to the bark on the tree trunk, pulled herself to her feet, and began to climb the tree limbs. Higher and higher she went, until she knew the massive bear wouldn't be able to reach her. She made the mistake of looking down and felt herself teeter when she saw how far away the ground was. She clutched the smaller branch at chest height, and wrapped her arms around it. She was too scared to move. She had her eyes closed and couldn't look down again. She knew vertigo would take over and she would fall if she did. April had always been afraid of heights, but the thought of being ripped apart and ending up the bear's dinner had been more frightening.

April had no idea how long she had been up in the tree, but the loud, deep voice of a man below made her flinch with fear.

"You can come down now. I'm not going to hurt you," the male voice called.

"Go away," April's voice wavered in reply.

"Now, don't be like that. I just want to help you. Are you lost? Where is your family?"

"Please, just leave me alone."

"Come on, now. You can't stay up there all day and night. Do you want me to come and get you?"

"No! Oh God, please."

"Please what, honey?"

"Please…help me down?"

"What are you afraid of?"

"Heights. Okay. I'm scared to death of heights."

"Then what are you doing up there?"

"There was a big bear. I didn't want to end up being its dinner," April replied with a whimper.

"Don't move, honey. I'm coming up. What's your name?"

"April."

"Okay, April, I'm Ben Koku. I'll have you back down on the ground before you know it. What were you doing wandering around in the forest alone? Where are your mates?"

"I don't have any mates. I don't belong here at all. I was just trying to find my way back home. I don't even know where I am, or how I got here."

"Easy there, honey. Everything will be all right. Are you sure you don't have any mates?"

"Yes. No. I don't know."

"Well, which is it? Yes or no?" Ben asked as he climbed.

"Well, since I don't belong here, am not from this part of the world, then no, I don't believe I have any mates."

"That's not really an honest answer, is it, April?" Ben asked from the branch below her.

* * * *

The sight of the small female wandering in the forest alone had surprised Ben. The fact that she had been scared of his beast alerted him to the fact she was definitely not from their world. He wondered how she had arrived here.

"I'm going to come up on your branch now, honey. Then I'll get you down. Don't you worry about a thing, all right? I'll have you safe on the ground in no time at all," Ben stated, lifting himself up to the next branch with ease.

When he was standing behind April, he scented the claim her mates had made on her skin, but he didn't want to contradict her until he had her safely back on the ground. She was such a little thing. She barely reached his chest. Ben wrapped an arm around her waist to steady her when she turned her head to look at him. The sight of her sky-blue eyes, looking into his own, knocked the breath right out of him. She was so beautiful. She had creamy white skin and long, golden hair. Her scent was of vanilla and honey, which drew his beast to the surface. He had to physically wrestle his beast back down to stop it from taking over. He didn't want to scare the little female more than he already had.

"I'm going to hold on to you real tight, but I want you to turn around and face me. I need to get you onto my back, so I can get you down from here. Okay?" Ben asked quietly, breathing in her delectable scent. He felt his cock harden in his pants and knew he was in deep trouble. This little female was his mate, and by the scent near both sides of her neck, she had already been claimed by the two Alpha panthers. Shit, what was he going to do? He sniffed more deeply, but couldn't smell their seed on her. They hadn't had sex with her yet. Maybe he could persuade her to mate with him, as well. Once a mate bit his woman and then made love to her, there was no chance of anyone else claiming her. But since they hadn't planted their seed into her yet, Ben knew he could claim her, just as the two Alpha panthers had. He hoped like hell they didn't come looking for her before he got the chance.

April whimpered as she moved around carefully on the large tree branch. Ben held her tightly around the waist to keep her safe. He maneuvered her until she was standing in front of him, and he now had his back to the tree trunk. He made sure he had his balance and then let his other hand, holding on to another branch, release his hold. He picked April up into his arms, swung her around onto his back, and had to hold in a chuckle as she wrapped her arms around his neck and her legs around his waist. He heard her whimper as he began to climb down the tree.

"Keep your eyes closed, honey, that way you won't get vertigo and feel ill. I'll have you down in no time." Ben gave one of her thighs a quick, soothing rub.

Ben was three quarters of the way down the tree when he heard the roar of two furious Alpha panthers. He knew, without a doubt, they were on the prowl for their female and would also have any others of the panther clan out looking. Ben stopped, blowing out a breath of frustration. He was going to have to bite April now, to lay claim to her, as well, or he would never get the chance. He didn't want to scare her, though. He could already feel her trembling at the fury audible in the Alpha panthers' growls.

"That was them, wasn't it? They're looking for me. I don't know what to do. I just want to go home," April sobbed.

Ben sat down on the large branch he was standing on, pulled April around off his back, and sat her down on his lap so she was straddling him. She clutched her arms around his neck and cried in earnest. Her tears were heart wrenching. He wanted to wrap her up and take her away, but knew he would be in deep shit if he did. He ran a large hand up and down her back, soothing her, until she finally gave a last hiccup and stopped crying.

"I'm sorry. I didn't mean to cry all over you."

"Hey, don't worry about it, honey. You obviously had a lot of tension stored up you needed to get rid of. Now, I want you to listen to me, but don't interrupt until I've finished. We don't have much time before your mates are going to be here. I won't ever hurt you, so please don't be frightened of what I tell you, okay?" Ben asked.

* * * *

April gave Ben a tentative nod and looked up into his liquid brown eyes. He had the kind of eyes a person could drown in. He was such a handsome man. His dark-brown hair and whiskered cheeks and chin only added extra appeal. He had a warm, muscular chest and arms, and his thighs were small tree trunks, which rippled beneath her ass as he moved. His scent was so masculine she held her breath and kept it in her lungs as long as possible before she released it. April had no idea what was happening to her, but she was so horny she wanted to rip Ben's pants down and impale herself on his cock. She was turning into a nymphomaniac.

"I'm the bear you were scared of, honey. I wasn't going to hurt you. I was just curious. I wanted to find out who you were. Your scent drew me to you, April. You're my mate, as well," Ben explained.

"No. No. Oh shit. Let me go. Ben, please? I can't do this. I want to go home."

"April, listen to me, honey. Gage and Saxon will be here any minute. Will you let me claim you, as well? I can help you with those two Alpha panthers, especially Gage. He can be a real hard-ass. Saxon can, too, but I'm a lot more easygoing than they are. I think it's because I'm of the bear clan. We tend to be a lot more laid back than the panther clan. What do you say, honey? Will you let me claim you, too?"

"I don't know. I mean, I don't know how to handle one man, let alone two or three. Shit, I just don't know," April breathed out. Her life was beyond her control. She'd had two men claim her already, without her permission. How the hell could she cope with another one? At least he was asking, instead of just taking, the way Gage and Saxon had.

A low growl below them caused April to jump and shriek. She looked down to see two large black panthers staring at her through golden, glowing eyes. They were both pissed, and April knew that was an understatement. They were so furious she could almost see fire shooting out of their eyes at her and Ben.

"Answer, April. Now," Ben whispered quietly in her ear.

"Yes," April replied without looking at Ben. She was so scared of what she saw in one of the panther's eyes she began to shake. She just hoped letting Ben claim her, as well, was the right thing to do.

* * * *

Ben leaned his head down and sniffed at April's shoulder. He called on his beast and let his teeth elongate, then bit into her shoulder next to where one of the panthers had claimed her. He licked the drops of blood from her wound and groaned out loud as the taste of her life force erupted onto his taste buds. His cock throbbed and hardened even more in his pants. He had to struggle with his beast until he had it pushed back down and he was once more in control.

The roar of two panthers pulled him back to his surroundings, and he knew he was going to have a fight on his hands. He was about to place April safely on the tree limb then climb down to confront his two friends, but they beat him to it. They leapt up and were on the tree branch on either side of him and April before he could blink. He knew they wouldn't put April in danger, so he was quite happy to stay where he was for the moment.

He watched as Gage and Saxon changed back to human form. Gage reached over to April and plucked her out of Ben's arms. He heard her whimper with fear as she literally flew through the air but stopped when she landed on Gage's naked lap.

"What the fuck do you think you were doing, Ben? You knew we'd claimed April first. You had no right to claim her, as well!" Gage growled.

"Well, that's where you're wrong, buddy. I asked April. I actually gave her a choice, not like some others around here. Her answer was yes," Ben replied.

"Is that true, April?" Gage asked. Ben saw Gage place a large finger beneath her chin, raising her face to his.

"Yes," April replied belligerently. But she was clinging to Gage with her arms and legs, still afraid of being off the ground. Ben wanted her back in his arms so he could offer her comfort but knew Gage wouldn't relent in his present mood.

"Why? Why did you do that? You belong to us." Gage growled.

"I belong to no one. I am my own person. I am not a prize to be fought over. I am a human being with feelings. You scared the hell out of me, Gage. You and Saxon marked me, claimed me, without my consent. What are you going to do next? Are you going to offer me up to have sex with the rest of your men? I can't believe you made me enjoy what you did to me. I don't even know you. Now get me out of this fucking tree before I scream," April yelled.

"Honey, calm down. I don't want you falling. Come here and I'll get you down," Ben said, holding his arms out to her.

Ben heard April sob and saw her push against Gage's chest, trying to get him to release her. He nearly laughed at her feistiness when Gage he didn't let go. She punched him on the chest as hard as she could, but it didn't seem to faze Gage at all. By the way she shook her hand, Ben could tell she only ended up hurting her own knuckles. April held her arms out to Ben, and he pulled her over to his lap, challenging Gage with his glare. Ben swung her over onto his back and began the rest of the climb down to the ground.

Once they were on the ground again, Ben swung April around into his arms, cradling her against his chest, trying to comfort her. He knew it was going to be a fight to get her, Gage, and Saxon together, but he was determined to make it happen. He intended to woo April and then bring Gage and Saxon into their relationship. He knew he was going to have his work cut out. He would need to get Gage and Saxon alone and explain his plans. He had a feeling he could use Saxon, as well, in trying to tame their mate, since she had only said Gage had scared her. She didn't seem adverse to Gage's younger brother. In fact, if he was correct, and he knew he was, April was covertly watching the two Alphas from the panther clan, and from what he could see, she was looking at them with hunger in her eyes.

Chapter Four

April was outraged to find herself back where she had virtually started. She was back in the room of the palatial mansion, with the huge canopied bed and luxurious bathroom. If it wasn't for the fact she now had food, water, and the amenities she so desperately needed, she would have thrown a temper tantrum the size of a mountain.

April sighed, sat down at the table located near the large window, and picked at the food someone had thoughtfully left for her. She wondered where Ben, Gage, and Saxon were, but then pushed them from her mind. Gage had scared the absolute living shit out her when he had changed into his panther form. She had been so scared of his beast and knew neither she nor Saxon would have been able to stop him, not that she had really wanted to. She was very wary of him now and knew it would be a long time before she trusted him. She picked up her third glass of water and guzzled it down. She was still replacing the fluids she had lost while wandering in the rain forest. She pushed her plate of food aside just as the doors to her room opened. She turned her head and saw Ben heading toward her.

"Hey, honey. How are you feeling?" Ben asked, placing a kiss on her cheek. He pulled out the chair opposite her and sat down, studying her intently.

"Okay, I guess."

"What can I do to help you, April?"

"Help me find a way to go home. I don't belong here, Ben. This place is so different from where I come from."

"How so?"

"I live in a city, Ben. I work at a small publishing company and earn my own living. I'm independent. I can't stay here, can't you see that? I'll never belong in this place."

"Come here, honey," Ben stated, holding a hand out toward April.

April stood and walked around the table to Ben. She took his hand in hers, and he gently pulled her down onto his lap. She heard Ben sigh as she curled up on his lap and burrowed her face into his bare chest. She kissed his chest spontaneously. She wasn't as inimical to any of them as she tried to make out. But there was no way in hell she was giving in to them too easily. Especially Gage. He'd made her so mad when he had licked her pussy in his beast form. Ben sat holding her for a long time. She felt safe and content in his arms and didn't want to get up. Her eyelids were heavy, and she was so tired. She closed her eyes and gave in to her weariness.

April woke up in the dead of night. She was plastered up against Ben. Her pussy was aching, and she had one of her legs over his crotch. She could feel his long, thick erection throbbing against her in response. She slowly began to ease her leg off of him, then began to inch her way to the side of the bed. She didn't get far, because Ben tightened the arm he had wrapped around her waist and pulled her back against him. She gave up the struggle of trying to move away from him. She lay awake listening to the comforting beat of his heart against her ear and feeling the heat of his body wrapped around her own. She had never felt so safe and secure in her entire life.

April knew she was falling for Ben, and in a big way, but she knew she couldn't stay here. She didn't belong here. She had her life waiting for her, back in her own world. She had her own space, was independent, and answered to no one. She had never been so alone or lonely in her life. April's eyelids eventually became too heavy to keep open. She gave up the struggle and let sleep overtake her once more as she slipped into an erotic dream.

Large, warm hands were stroking her body, creating a heat so fierce, she was afraid she would erupt into flames if the fire building in her wasn't doused. Hands kneaded her breasts until she arched up into the pleasure they were giving her. She moaned in her throat, begging for more of the desirous sensations running through her body, from her breast down to the throbbing, wet core of her pussy. Fingers plucked at her hard nipples, shooting electric sparks straight to her clit and womb, making her muscles clench uselessly, her pussy begging to be filled. A warm, wet tongue laved over one of her sensitive nipples, making her arch up to get more contact with the pleasure-inducing appendage. The mouth drew on her hard, sucking her nipple in between warm, moist lips. Teeth bit down on her gently, holding her nipple still, while the tongue flickered back and forth across the surface, making her cry out with pleasure and need.

Another mouth took her other breast into its depths, giving her the decadence of having both her breasts pleasured at the same time. She felt large, warm palms run up the inside of her thighs, sliding up and down, getting closer and closer to the juncture of her legs. April bucked her hips up, needing to be touched, the fire raging in her body needing to be quenched. She sighed with relief when she felt that large, warm hand cup her mound, relieving a small amount of her throbbing need. Fingers separated her labia, and then one of them dipped into the well of her dripping, creamy hole. That same finger slid up between the slick folds of her cunt until it reached the top of her slit, massaging around and around her clit but never giving her what she needed most. She growled with frustration in the back of her throat and bucked her hips up, trying to get that finger to touch her aching clitoris. She heard a masculine chuckle, but didn't give it another thought. She was too far gone. She needed to be touched, needed her pussy to be filled, and was determined to get what she wanted.

April slowly opened her eyes to find herself surrounded by all three men. Her body was out of control. Her vagina was clenching, her juices dripping from her, making her thighs and ass wet. She looked down the length of her body to see Gage staring up at her waiting for her approval, and when she gave a small nod, his fingers began massaging her pussy, and his head was only inches away from her hot cunt. He didn't move. April knew he was waiting for her to move away from him, or to yell at him, even though she had just given him permission to touch her. When she didn't move or speak, he slid his fingers down through her pussy lips, slowly pushing one of his large, thick fingers up into her cunt. She turned her head when she saw movement at her sides near her chest. Ben and Saxon were lying on either side of her, not touching her, just waiting for her to decide what she wanted. When she relaxed her head back on the pillow beneath and closed her eyes, she knew she was in for a wild ride.

"Please, touch me," April sobbed, giving them permission to take her body where they wanted to lead.

April couldn't hold back the moan building in her throat as Gage bent down to her pussy and breathed over her hot, wet flesh. She felt goose bumps rise up over her skin, making her nipples pucker and stand up even further, just begging to be touched. Saxon and Ben leaned over her. One of them took a hard nipple into his mouth and sucked on her to the point of pain, while a finger and thumb plucked at her other elongated nub. She opened her eyes just as Ben took her mouth beneath his own, opening her lips using the firm pressure of his own lips. He thrust his tongue into her mouth, tasting every nook and cranny of her cavern, not leaving one inch of her untasted. He slid his tongue along hers then curled his muscle around her tongue, drawing it from her mouth into his and suckling on her flesh.

April moaned, unable to prevent the sound from escaping as Gage ran his sandpaper-textured tongue over her clit, swirling around the little bundle of sensitive nerves protruding out, eager for more. She had never felt so small and feminine, so sexy, so needed and wanted. She knew she shouldn't be letting them do this to her, but it had been so long since she had been touched, held. In fact, she couldn't remember the last time she'd had any kind of contact with another human being, besides verbally. She needed to feel needed, like she never had been before. She pushed the thoughts from her mind, letting the pleasure she was receiving from three of the sexiest, most masculine, dominant men she had ever met take her over.

They were consuming her. Gage was lapping at her clit as he slid a finger in and out of her wet sheath. He was torturing her with pleasure. The movement of his thrusting finger was so slow, April sobbed out her frustration. Saxon was sucking and plucking at her nipples, and Ben was ravishing her mouth. April could feel the beginning warning signs of an impending climax, so she thrust her hips at Gage's mouth, urging him to give her what she wanted, needed. April's womb began to coil into a tight spring as the three men claiming her as their mate played her body like a violin. The coil gathered in on itself, getting tighter and tighter, pulling the muscles in her abdomen and thighs rigid. When she thought she wouldn't be able to stand anymore, thinking she was about to snap, all movement ceased. Their hands and mouths withdrew from her tautly coiled body.

April screamed with rage, bounded up from her back to her knees with a lightning move. She pushed Gage back on the bed, catching him off guard by the surprised look on his face. She grabbed his massive prick in a firm grip, straddled his hips, and impaled herself on his hard shaft. He was so big she was only able to get a quarter of him inside her. Gage grabbed her around the waist, pulled her down to his chest, tilted her face up to his, and stared into her eyes. The heat, hunger, in his eyes was so potent, April felt singed by it. He lifted his head to her and possessed her mouth with his own. The kiss was so carnal, she felt like she was burning up from the inside out. As he devoured her mouth, he began to thrust his hips up into hers, holding her firmly, pulling her hips down to meet his own. Gage stopped intermittently, giving her time to adjust to his penetration, but she wanted none of that.

April began using her legs. She slid up and down his hard, thick shaft, pushing harder and harder until he was completely filling her cunt. April moaned out loud at the burning feel of his hard cock stretching her to the point of pain. She relished the feeling of being filled as she had never been filled before. She was in heaven and hell, needing to move, but wanting to savor the feel of his hard rod separating her tight muscles. She couldn't wait anymore. She had to move, and she had to do it now.

April began to ride Gage's cock like there was no tomorrow. She was totally out of control but didn't care. She wanted to feel her flesh gripping around his hard shaft as she reached orgasm, so she picked up her pace until her ass was slapping into his hard, muscular thighs. She needed to take the edge off of her fire, before she burned alive.

* * * *

Gage couldn't believe the wild woman who had just jumped him. April had been fighting him and Saxon, keeping them at arm's length. Something had changed, and now she was like a female panther in heat. She was now slamming herself down on his rock-hard, pulsing shaft. He wanted to stop her and savor the feeling of her flesh gripping his own tightly. He couldn't hold back the moan as she plunged down onto his cock again. The friction of her wet flesh sliding over his hard, pulsating shaft was nearly more than he could stand. He gripped her hips and held her down on his cock, not letting go as she tried to rise up again. He pulled her body down over his until she was covering him from chest to the tops of his thighs. He spread his legs wide, taking hers with him, giving Saxon or Ben access to her ass. Gage knew the three of them would all have to join their bodies with April's together to make their claim on her work to its proper completion. He knew he could be a selfish bastard and not let Ben join April's body with him and his brother, but he had a feeling a greater force was at work here. He just didn't know what. Even though he knew it was possible for more than one kind of shape-shifter to be able to claim a woman, it was very rare for different species to be able to claim a mate once she was claimed by another, even if they hadn't marked her with their seed, as well.

Gage saw Saxon give Ben the advantage of being able to take April's ass. He knew if it was him, he wouldn't have been so selfless. He wondered why his brother was giving Ben the first opportunity of burying his cock in their mate's little pucker. He didn't ask, though. For the Goddess truth, he was having trouble just breathing. April had claimed his voice when she had claimed his flesh. Gage watched as Ben produced a bowl of fragrant oil, which had been left on the table. He watched his bond mate place the bowl on the table beside the large bed then strip his clothes from his body. All the while, Gage was trying to keep April from squirming up and down on his cock.

* * * *

Ben dipped his fingers into the oil and coated his massive cock. The throbbing in his cock was so bad, the ache made him want to plunge his hard length into their mate and ride her hard and fast to completion. But he knew he was going to have to be gentle with their mate, so he took a few deep breaths, releasing them slowly as he tried to regain control of his rampant desire. Once his cock was coated liberally, he dipped two of his fingers into the bowl of oil once more, moved up onto the bed behind April, and slowly began to massage her little, dark pucker. He nearly shot his wad when April sobbed with pleasure from the touch of his finger to her ass. Ben breathed evenly and deeply as he massaged the sensitive hole of her anus and gave a growl of approval when her little hole relaxed and opened up to him. Ben pushed the tip of one finger into April's ass and held still as her muscles clamped down onto his digit like a vise. He began to pump his thick finger in and out of her hole, spreading the lubricating oil over her internal walls by wiggling his finger around as he slid it in and out a few times. He slowly withdrew his finger again, dipped into the bowl for more oil, and then began to push two fingers into his mate's ass. She opened up to his penetration as she tried to buck back onto his fingers. He moved his other arm around her waist to hold her steady. He pumped his fingers in and out of her ass until her muscles were used to his invasion and her asshole opened up some more. He pushed those fingers into her canal all the way, then began to scissor his fingers, stretching her tight anal muscles. When April began rocking her hips back and forth, he withdrew his fingers from her hole. Looking down at her heart-shaped ass opened wide for him was such a turn-on. He thrust three fingers into her anus, pumping them in and out, spreading his fingers once more to help stretch her.

The sight of his own fingers moving in and out of her tight hole was nearly his undoing. He released his arm from around her waist, grabbed onto his large balls, and gave them a sharp tug. The pain was just enough of a bite to hold off his impending climax. Ben grasped his dick in his hand, aligned it with April's asshole, and began to push into her body. He had to push hard to get the tip of his cock through the tight ring of muscles of her sphincter, and he couldn't hold in his moan of pleasure as his cockhead popped through those tightly clasping muscles. He grabbed his balls again, giving them another sharp tug, breathing in and out deeply as he tried to control his raging lust. Once he had his body back under control, he slowly but surely pushed into his mate's anus until he was buried balls-deep. He wrapped his arm around her waist again, holding her back against his chest as he moved her to a sitting position between himself and Gage.

The sight and sound of his mate bucking and moaning between him and Gage had his cock pulsing in her tight, gripping flesh. She was sobbing between them, tears streaming down over her beautifully flushed cheeks as she begged him and Gage for more.

* * * *

"Oh my God. What are you doing to me? Move, damn it. Please, fuck me," April yelled at them as she wiggled and bucked, trying to get the men to move.

She spied Saxon moving toward her from her peripheral vision and gasped in awe at the size of his cock and his sculpted, masculine body. He was an Adonis, but she was also afraid of the gigantic size of him. He was large all over, but she knew his brother was even bigger. Every thought left her mind as he crawled up onto the bed beside her. He knelt down close to her, grasped her hair with one of his hands, and began to pull her head toward his crotch.

"Take me in your mouth, mate. Suck my cock," Saxon growled out at her.

April eyed his cock with trepidation, knowing there was no way in hell she would be able to take anything of him besides the tip. He was so wide and long, she knew she would be unable to take him without pain to her jaw. She eyed the slit in the top of his cock. A pearl of clear fluid was bubbling up out and began to slowly slide down over his cockhead. April didn't think. She flicked her tongue out and swirled it over the top of his cock, tasting his creamy essence for the first time. The taste of his fluid was enough to send her into a frenzy of desire again, the flavor of his salty yet sweet cum drawing her to taste more of him. She opened her mouth as wide as she could and began to force her way down onto his large appendage. She couldn't get more than a quarter of his massive size into her mouth and moaned out her disappointment. It didn't seem to bother Saxon, though. He held her head still by gripping her hair tighter and closer to the base of her skull and began to slowly pump his hips.

As Saxon got into a slow, steady rhythm of fucking her mouth, Gage and Ben began to move her hips back and forth between them. The glide and slide of their flesh in and out of her body made perspiration form on her body in a light sheen and pleasure radiate out from all three of her holes. She was in heaven and hell. They were moving too slowly for her liking, and she tried to rock her hips back and forth between them, faster and harder. She growled out in frustration when they wouldn't let her control her own or their movements in and out of her body.

"Do that again, baby," Saxon demanded as he shoved his cock

into her mouth a little more.

April couldn't ask him what he meant with his cock stuffed into her mouth, so she raised an eyebrow in query, looking up into his eyes.

"Moan on my cock again, baby. It feels so good. The vibration of from your voice enhances my pleasure," Saxon explained.

April didn't need to be told twice, and since Gage and Ben had picked up the pace of their pumping hips a little more, she couldn't contain her moan of pleasure and approval. With every forward thrust of the three men's hips, they went a little faster and deeper. One of the men fucking her ass and pussy was always filling one of her holes as the other withdrew in a pleasure-inducing slide of flesh in flesh. April felt the heaviness in her lower abdomen increase, her pussy dripping her juices from her grasping flesh as Gage, Ben, and Saxon slid in and out of her holes. She had never felt so submissively feminine in her life. The fact that her body and pleasure were in the control of the three men made her flames burn hotter, her cunt dripping more cream as the pace of their thrusting hips increased yet again.

April could feel her body beginning to coil tighter, fire permeating her from the top of her head to the tips of her toes. Her legs and toes began to tingle with warmth, molten lava spreading throughout her system, her body coiling tighter than a bow string. The sounds of the men fucking her as they groaned out their own pleasure made her so damn horny. Her pelvic floor muscles got tighter and tighter, gripping down on the hard cocks shuttling in and out of her ass and pussy. Ben moved one of his hands up to her breasts. He pinched one puckered nipple, then the other, as Gage moved a hand to the top of her pussy. He began to lightly caress her protruding clitoris, urging her towards her peak of completion. All of a sudden, the coil snapped, hurtling her up the side of a mountain to the peak, hurling her over the edge of the cliff. She screamed out her pleasure as her body gripped the massive cocks buried in her, clutching at them as if she would never let them out of her body again. Her body was a shaking, convulsing mass of nerves, the pleasure so intense her vision dimmed, stars dancing before her eyes. She felt her pussy gush out her release, covering herself and Gage with her climactic fluids. She heard Saxon's warning as if from far away, but her mind was able to comprehend what he had said.

"Swallow my cum, baby. Don't you lose a drop of it," Saxon stated, then roared out his own completion as he shot load after load of his seed down her throat, coating her tongue with his salty, sweet flavor.

April moved one of her hands to the middle of his penis, frowning when she felt a large bulge protruding from his flesh. It was like a large knot of flesh halfway up his shaft, which locked him inside her as he emptied his balls into her body, but she was too far gone to think straight. She swallowed again and again until he stopped shooting in her mouth, then licked him clean. She released his cock and slumped down onto Gage's chest, too drained to move her hips with them, until he and Ben reached their own culmination.

She heard Gage and Ben roar out their own climaxes, then shivered and quaked in their arms as she felt large knots of flesh protruding from the middle of their penises, as well, locking them together as their cum filled her body. Gage had told her this may happen with a mate, but he hadn't been sure. They were filling her full of their life giving sperm. It was their beasts' way of making sure none of their fertile semen escaped from their mate's body. The knots of flesh kept pulsing in her body, shocking her as they sent her up and over the edge once more. Her body released another spurt of cream right before she passed out from the pleasure consuming her body.

Chapter Five

April opened her eyes to find herself in the large bathing pool. Saxon held her on his lap as Ben and Gage washed her tired, sore body. Her muscles were aching from the strenuous workout they had just endured. She knew she shouldn't let them take such liberties with her, but she was too satiated to care. Once she was clean, Gage and Ben washed themselves, and then Saxon handed her over to Ben and washed his own body.

April castigated herself as she remembered she had literally jumped Gage's bones then let Ben and Saxon fuck her as well. She had only ever had one lover, and even though she had thought herself in love at the time, she knew she had just been another notch on the bastard's belt. She had never behaved like that before in her life. She had no idea what had come over her. She felt her cheeks heat with embarrassment, recalling what she had let them do to her.

Ben must have seen her expression, because he tilted her face up to his with a finger beneath her chin. "You have nothing to be ashamed of, honey. What we just did is natural between a claimed woman and her mates."

"It might be natural to you, but it's not to me." April pushed against his massive chest with her hands and turned her face away from him.

Ben didn't let April go until they had reached the steps leading from the bathing pool. She had to gather her courage before she was able to walk up the steps nonchalantly, over to the drying towels on a shelf, and then quickly wrap herself in the large, fluffy cloth. She knew all three of the men were watching her, the hair at her nape prickling with awareness. She pushed her shoulders back and sauntered from the room as regally as a queen would have. Once she was away from their perusing gazes, April dropped her facade of nonchalance, quickly dried herself off, and searched for her clothes. They were nowhere to be found. She scowled with frustration then went rummaging through all the drawers and closets trying to find something to wear. None of the clothes she found would fit her. There was a huge amount of the same black, leather-looking pants, and after holding a few of them up to her waist, noticing the legs of the pants were still trailing on the floor, she gave up the futility of even bothering to try them on. Besides, there were no tops to be seen, and there was no way in hell she was going to roam about the place half-naked. She sat down on the side of the bed and sighed, not knowing what she was going to do. She couldn't stay wrapped in a towel for the rest of her stay. Just as she was pondering her dilemma, the big double doors to the bedroom opened. A tall woman with slanting green eyes, long black hair, and such a beautiful face entered the room. April had to bite her tongue to keep the gasp of awe from escaping her mouth at the sight of the beautiful woman.

"I have some clothes for you," the woman spat at April.

"Thanks. What's your name?"

"What gives you the right to question me, you little bitch? You are not even from this plane of existence. I should change into my beast and shred you into little pieces."

April eyed the malicious woman in front of her, wondering what her beef was. She decided not to say anything more, knowing her silence would eventually get to the vindictive woman.

The woman moved toward April with an unconscious grace, making her feel a tad jealous of her. She eyed the woman and watched as she threw some clothes at April. April caught them reflexively, not bothering to thank the bitch a second time.

"I will be waiting for you to slip up. I know you will, and when you're not looking, I will kill you with my bare hands. If it wasn't for you, those men would be mine. They were mine before you ever arrived on the scene, and they will be again. Best watch your back, little human, because I will win in the end."

April just stared at the woman, not wanting to give her the satisfaction of seeing her wariness. The woman turned away from her then quickly turned back. April tried not to cringe away from the evil intent in her eyes, but knew she hadn't been successful in hiding her fear when the woman smirked. She was about to turn away from her again, when she moved closer to April once more. She gripped April's long blonde hair in a fist and gave it a vicious tug. The woman then proceeded to spit in April's face.

April felt all the fear and uncertainness she had felt over the last twenty-four hours or so culminate into pure fury. She stood up slowly as she glared at the woman who had done such a disgusting thing to her. She didn't let the woman's size or the fact she could change shape intimidate her. April was so furious she was shaking. She reached up, tugged her hair from the woman's grasp, and slapped her across the face with all her strength. The woman let out a sharp cry of pain, staggering back away from April only to land on her ass on the floor. April moved until she was standing over the woman, grasped the woman's hair in a fist, and wrapped it around her wrist, pulling on it as hard as she could.

"Just because I'm human, you little bitch, doesn't mean I can't take you on," April ground out through clenched teeth.

"April, what the hell are you doing?" Gage bellowed, moving toward her quickly. He took April's hand in his own and squeezed hard. "Let Vanessa go, now."

When April didn't immediately comply, he squeezed her wrist harder until she had no choice but to let the bitch's hair go. He released her when he saw her wince with pain, and she knew he hadn't meant to hurt her. She looked up into his eyes and saw the anger he was portraying to her, as well as regret for hurting her.

"I'm sorry, April, I didn't mean to hurt you," Gage said quietly.

She didn't acknowledge his apology. She was too hurt emotionally. He hadn't even asked what the problem was, just assumed that it was all her fault. That sent a stab of pain piercing into her chest and heart. It was more distressing than the pain he had inflicted on her wrist. He obviously thought she was the one being the bitch. She decided she wasn't going to enlighten him. She didn't care what Gage, Saxon, or Ben thought of her. She watched without emotion as Gage helped the sobbing Vanessa to her feet then cuddled her against his chest as he glared at April. Vanessa had her back to Saxon and Ben, her face half buried in Gage's chest as he tried to placate the upset woman. April saw the malicious, satisfied smirk she sent in April's direction.

April turned her back on the woman, grabbed the clothes from the bed, and headed back to the bathing room. April removed the towel and pulled on the short, leather-type skirt and top, which left her midriff bare. She tugged and pulled, knowing her efforts were futile. No amount of tugging was going to lengthen the skirt or the top. She sighed in resignation, then sat down on the marble bench and pulled on the black, knee-high boots, surprised to find they fit her feet and were quite comfortable. April knew that bitch, Vanessa, had been right about one thing. She didn't belong here, and she was determined to find her way home again.

April walked out of the large bathroom, hoping the three men claiming to be her mates had left the room. She was out of luck. They were still there. She walked over to the small table in front of the window, sat down, and stared outside, taking in the beautifully landscaped gardens stretched out before her as far as she could see. She couldn't wait to get away from her so-called mates. She wanted nothing more to do with them. They didn't even trust her. How the hell could anyone build a relationship when there was no trust? As far as she was concerned, love and trust were the basis to every solid relationship.

April couldn't believe what she was thinking. Why was she

worried about whether her mates trusted her not? She didn't even like them, for goodness' sake. And she wasn't going to be here long enough to be worried about needing their trust or love. She was going to find a way home if it was the last thing she did.

"April, look at me," Gage demanded.

April was still feeling too hurt to be bothered with her mates, so she just continued to stare out the window ignoring them.

A firm hand grabbed hold of her chin, pulling her to face Gage. April made sure to keep her face totally blank of any feelings and expressions. She just stared up at him passively, not showing any concern at all.

"What the hell did you think you were doing to Vanessa? Do you think you are going to make any friends by treating people that way? What is wrong with you, woman? I should put you over my knee and tan your ass until it's red and raw. If I ever catch you treating another person that way again, that's just where you're going to find yourself. Just because you're my mate doesn't mean you can be disrespectful to my people. I want you to think about what you have done. When you can find a bit of remorse for your actions, you will go and apologize to Vanessa. Is that understood?" Gage asked.

April didn't respond to him at all. She didn't even blink. She just stared through him. She ignored him totally. She was so hurt inside she didn't think she could ever forgive him. How could he believe she would do something like that without provocation? He let her chin go when she continued to ignore him. She saw Gage turn on his heel and storm out of the room. Saxon was frowning down at her, too. No doubt he was just as angry with her, as well. He didn't bother to ask her what had been going on with her and Vanessa. He spun on his heel and walked toward the door. He paused for a moment, turned back, and called for Ben to follow him.

Ben surprised her as he gave her a kiss on the cheek then went hurrying after Saxon. The sound of the large timber doors closing behind him was what she needed to hear. She had been on the point of breaking down in front of her mates, and that was the last thing she wanted to do. It seemed the only thing she had left was her pride, and she would damn well hold on to that. They weren't going to take that away from her, as well.

April sighed as the tension she had held on to slowly left her body. She wanted nothing more than to break down and have a good cry, but she was determined not to give in. She wanted to get outside. Maybe the tranquility of the gardens would help soothe her ragged nerves. She only hoped she could find her way out.

April was surprised to see two tall, muscular men standing guard at her door. She didn't bother to acknowledge them. She knew they were there to watch over her. She didn't really care at the moment. In fact, her anger was finally receding, and she was beginning to feel totally numb inside. She meandered down the long hallway, and when she once again came to the *T* intersection, she turned left, trying to find her way outside. She found the glass doors midway down the long corridor, opened them, and stepped out into the warm, humid air.

April breathed in the scents of blooming flowers as she wandered up and down gravel footpaths. The gardens were gorgeous, hedges surrounding the perimeters to separate the beds from the pathways. She wandered for hours, breathing in the scents, listening to the cheerful chirping of birds and the peaceful, soothing sound of water trickling somewhere nearby. April had always loved water in gardens. It seemed to have such a soothing effect on her nerves. She followed the sound until she found herself in the center of the landscaped gardens and sat down on a bench, which was shaded by the branches and leaves of a large tree. She watched what looked to be goldfish swimming lazily in the deep, wide pond as they foraged for food. She had no idea how long she sat there staring at the fish as she tried to work out a way to escape from this luxurious palace.

April looked around her, trying to see where her guards were hiding. She couldn't see them anymore and wondered if she had lost them as she meandered around the gardens or whether they had been called away for some other duty. She rose from the bench and began to move toward the far side of the gardens, away from the palace. She was hopeful she would be able to escape since she wasn't being closely watched at the moment.

April realized the gardens and palace grounds weren't even fenced in and felt excitement permeate her body. She cautiously looked around her, trying to spot her guards. She didn't hesitate to keep walking when they were nowhere in sight. She had no idea where she was going, or even if she was heading in the right direction. She just knew she couldn't stay here any longer. She knew she was going to have to move quickly. She didn't want it to be discovered she was missing too soon. She was going to need a large head start, because she knew her mates would have no trouble tracking her, whatever time of day or night it was. They could easily shift into their beast forms and be on her before she knew it.

April ran through the forest, not stopping when her legs began to burn or a stitch formed in her side. She was panting heavily, but knew she had to keep going. She didn't want to be where she wasn't wanted or trusted. Pain sliced through her chest again at Gage's lack of trust, and her heart felt wounded with betrayal. She bit her lip as tears coursed down her cheeks. She knew there could only be one reason for her to feel such pain. She was beginning to have feelings for him, for all of them. She loved the fact that Gage was so arrogant and dominant. He knew what he wanted and went after it. She loved that he wanted her, needed her so much. He drew her to him with his displays of masculinity. Saxon was just a dominant as Gage, but he was a lot gentler than his brother and went about getting what he wanted differently. And Ben, her gentle giant, was already embedded in her heart. She knew deep down she wanted to let go and be the submissive to their dominance, but she didn't know if she could trust them enough.

She hadn't felt pain like this when she had found out her previous lover had only wanted to fuck her, not really have a relationship with her. She had dated that bastard for six months before she had given her body to him. Yet, she knew it had been her pride that had been wounded, not her heart. She had to get out of here, and the faster, the better. There was no way she would be able to hide her feelings from her mates forever, and the last thing she wanted was to see the satisfaction in their eyes at knowing they had a hold of her, without returning her feelings. She'd been there once before, or thought she had, but she knew now the pain she had felt at having her pride wounded was nothing compared to having her heart broken by her mates.

April didn't see the trap covered by leaves on the ground. One moment she was jogging along, tears blurring her vision, and the next her feet were being pulled from beneath her body. She found herself hanging upside down about ten feet from the ground. Her body was still swaying and spinning back and forth, and she had to close her eyes so she could try and keep the nausea she was feeling at bay. When the ropes holding her captive around the ankles finally stopped spinning, April was able to open her eyes. She slammed them shut again as vertigo set in, making her feel dizzy because of the height she was from the ground.

April knew she was going to have to try and free herself once she had her vertigo under control, and if she couldn't manage it, then she was going to have to start yelling for help. The last thing she needed was to feel humiliation when her mates found her hanging upside down in a trap. April didn't know it would be so difficult to use her stomach muscles to pull herself up until she could reach her ankles from her upside-down position. She was quite a fit person and had always done stomach crunches in her normal exercise routine. It took more out of her than she expected, leaving her panting for breath as she gripped the rope in one of her hands as she caught her breath again.

April knew if she was able to loosen the ropes around her ankles, she would then end up having to contend with a drop of at least ten feet to the ground below. She didn't really know if she was capable of such a feat, but knew she didn't have much of a choice. If she wanted to escape before her mates found her, she needed to get out of this trap, now. April studied the knots and loops binding her in midair but couldn't see a way to remove them from her ankles. She was going to need two hands to pry her feet out of the ropes, which meant she was going to need all the strength of her stomach muscles to hold herself in her current position. If she could manage to get one of her feet out of the trapping rope, the second one would follow easily.

April tugged and pulled at the loop binding her ankles until the palms of her hands were feeling raw and burnt from the abrasive rope. She knew she was defeated, as the weight of her body was keeping the rope taut. They wouldn't move an inch, no matter how hard she tugged and pulled. April was panting with exertion, and her stomach muscles were screaming at her to be released from their strenuous exercise. She gripped the rope with her grazed, burning palms, letting her stomach muscles relax with a groan. She carefully followed the rope up to the tree branch until she could see where the rope was wrapped around the large limb several times, then around the large tree trunk. She was fucked. There was no way she would be able to get down by herself.

Chapter Six

"What do you mean you lost her?" Gage roared at the two guards he had ordered to follow his mate around.

"She was in the gardens sitting at the pond, Sire. She didn't even seem to be aware of us. She just sat on the bench staring at the pond. I only left her for a brief moment to relieve myself, and by the time I got back, she was gone," one of the guards explained.

Gage studied the two guards who had been appointed to protect their mate. They were still quite young and not yet fully trained warriors. He wondered why he had not thought of this before and had more seasoned warriors protect his mate.

"Where were you while this knucklehead was relieving himself?" Saxon asked.

Gage took another step forward and stopped in front of the young warriors.

"Um, I...I was just...I was with my girlfriend, Sire," the man answered, his face a bright crimson.

"Let me get this straight," Ben stated quietly. "While you were fucking your girlfriend and you were taking a piss, our mate was either kidnapped or escaped from the palace grounds. Is that about right?"

"Yes, sir." The young men mumbled their timid replies.

"You will address Ben as Sire, too. He is your elder, and he is also Alpha of the bear clan. Is that understood?" Gage snapped out.

"Yes, Sire," they answered Gage. "Sorry, Sire," they apologized as they turned to Ben.

"I want you two bumbling idiots to report to Jasper first thing in the morning. You are to train with our warrior trainer until you have learned what a good warrior should know. Now get out of my sight before I kill you both," Gage roared.

Gage watched the two young warriors bow to the three of them then rush out of the room. They nearly crashed into the doorway in their eagerness to escape the displeasure of their Alphas.

"Saxon, go and round up ten of our best warriors. I want their help in tracking our mate. We may need to fight to get our mate back, if she has been taken by another kind. We'll meet at the pond in the gardens. The warriors should be able to catch our mate's scent from there," Gage stated.

Saxon turned to do his brother's bidding as Gage led Ben out into the yard. Gage followed the meandering path their mate had made through the gardens until they came to the pond in the center. April's scent was still quite prevalent, for which Gage was thankful. The older warriors would definitely be able to help them with the search for their mate. Gage and Ben paced restlessly until they heard the warriors coming toward them.

"Thank you for coming so quickly. I know you have other chores you have had to neglect at my request," Gage began. "Our mate has gone missing, and I'm not sure if she was kidnapped or has tried to escape, yet again. I am fearful she may have stumbled on other were kinds and want you to back us up if we have to fight to get our mate back. I cannot scent any other odor here besides our mates, so I am sure she has just tried to escape again. I want you all to get her scent into your lungs and noses from near the bench, so you will be able to help us track her. If we find her and she is alone, I do not want any of you to intervene as I punish our mate. Is that understood?"

"Yes, Sire," the ten warriors replied without hesitation.

"All right, let's head out," Saxon stated and took the lead in tracking their mate's scent, Gage and Ben close behind with the ten large warriors following.

Gage followed the scent of his mate. Even if he hadn't been able to scent her, it wouldn't have been hard to track her, because she had left an easy trail to follow. She obviously had no skills on how to hide her presence from others. Sometimes her footsteps were clearly visible in the damp earth on the ground. Other signs were broken twigs and scattered leaves she had disturbed, which showed bugs scurrying to bury themselves to hide beneath the fallen foliage once more. Gage knew from the length between her footsteps and the heavier impressions that their mate had literally been running away. He was quite surprised that such a small woman could have traveled so far in so little time. She had only been missing for the better part of an hour, and they had traveled quite a few miles and still had not caught up with her.

The loud, piercing female scream echoing through the forest made Gage, his brother, and Ben sprint toward the vicinity from which the noise had come. He stopped in surprise as he spied his mate hanging upside down in a trap, staring in horror at the huge lion crouching on a large tree limb, watching her as if she was going to be a delectable meal.

* * * *

April's body began to shake uncontrollably when she saw the large lion staring at her as if she was its dinner. She wasn't sure if it was a shifter or the real thing, but had no real desire to find out. She kept her gaze on the animal and screamed as loud as she could, hoping someone would find her before she became its meal. She watched the lion leap away to another tree then disappear from sight. She let her body release the tension that had gripped it, relief making her close her eyes. She knew she had just had a lucky escape and prayed to God someone would come and help her down from her trap.

April opened her eyes when she heard movement below her, then snapped them shut again as she saw the furious frowns on the faces of her mates. She knew she was in deep shit and really only had herself to blame for the predicament she currently found herself in. Then she thought back to the morning and how Vanessa, then Gage, had treated her. She let the hurt she had felt consume her and turned the emotion into anger. There was no way in hell she was going to let them berate her when she had been driven to run away.

April watched as Ben climbed the tree until he had reached the rope trapping her. She watched as he held the rope in one hand, then saw claws protrude from the tips of his fingers on his other hand. He swiped his claws through the rope, cutting it, which sent April swinging through the air. She was heading straight for the tree and knew she was going to end up bruised and battered when she impacted with it. She closed her eyes and held her hands out in front of her, hoping to lessen the impact. She opened her eyes in surprise when she was caught in a firm, steady grip.

Saxon had grabbed her by her waist when she swung toward him. He held her still to steady her then swung her up and over his shoulder. He began to climb down the tree without taking the time to release the ropes binding her ankles together. Once he was on the ground, he swung her off his shoulder and held her cradled firmly against his chest. April was too scared to look up at him or Gage, so she kept her eyes lowered as she watched them from beneath the cover of her eyelashes. Gage frowned down at her as he removed the ropes binding her ankles, and then he pulled her boots from her feet. He held her feet still as he studied the grazed, red skin around her ankles.

April tried to push his hands away, but he just gave them a slight admonishing tap and kept up his perusal. She was about to push him away again but was stopped as Ben came up to her and Saxon's side. He took her hands into his own larger ones and studied her raw palms. She flinched when Gage and Saxon growled loudly and Ben let out a large roar of his own. She tried to cover her fear by struggling to be free again. She turned her head away from them, and that was when she noticed the group of men scowling at her from a few feet away.

God, was she never able to do anything right? It didn't matter what she did or didn't do, she was the one everyone seemed to blame. Well, maybe she should just let them. Why the hell should she care what anyone else thought of her, or believed her to be guilty of? She had done nothing wrong. They were the ones who had betrayed her, and Gage was the worse culprit of them all.

April was at the end of her tether, and to find the group of men scowling at her, as well, was the last straw. She had never even met them, so why should they be so pissed at her? They had no justification as far as she was concerned. She pulled her hands away from Ben, kicked her legs, and wiggled until she began to slide down Saxon's body to the ground. He released her when her bare feet hit the ground and took a step back from her when she scowled at him and then Gage and Ben.

"I am not going back with you. You are going to help me get back to my own home," April yelled at the men standing in front of her. She had to tilt her head back quite a ways so she could see their eyes. She was getting a pain in her neck but was not about to show any sign of weakness. She was going to let them have it with both barrels until they knew how displeased she was with them, especially Gage.

"No, we are not. You are our mate. You will live in our home and do as you are told," Gage rapped out.

"Why the fucking hell should I? You don't trust me at all, do you? Why should I take orders or listen to you, when you don't want to hear anything I have to say? You are such a fucking hypocrite. I don't even like you. None of you have done anything to gain my trust or given me your trust in return. All you want is someone you can fuck then discard when you've finished. Well, I am not going to be used that way. I will not be a convenient receptacle for your seed. I am not a broodmare. You can go back to your precious Vanessa and fuck her all you want. I think if you ever touch me again I would be physically sick." April was gasping for breath when she finally finished her tirade. She had been so full of anger at their treatment of her, which had made her ire consume her and take over. She couldn't actually remember what she had just said, but knowing herself, it hadn't been pleasant.

"How did you know we had been with Vanessa before we found you?" Saxon asked quietly.

"Oh, so now you're interested in what happened with that bitch. I don't know whether I should give you the satisfaction of answering you, but maybe if I do you will understand how I work. I would never, ever hurt anyone without provocation. That bitch had great delight in telling me that you belonged to her. She said I was nothing, because I wasn't even from your plane. When I didn't retaliate or even answer her back, she grabbed a handful of my hair and spat in my face. Of course, now I know she deliberately provoked me into retaliating, and that is what you caught me doing when you found me standing over that vicious bitch with her hair in my hand. You didn't even ask me what was wrong," April yelled when Gage nodded his head, contradicting her. "You asked me what in God's name I thought I was doing, then you crushed my wrist under your hand, using your brute strength to get me to let go of that bitch. You comforted her, and while she was crying those crocodile tears to get your sympathy, she was smirking at me with disdain. Well, as far as I'm concerned, you can just go and fuck yourself." April spun on her heels and began to walk away. She didn't want the men to see the tears in her eyes. She didn't want to stay here and be treated like a second-class citizen. She wanted to go back to her boring little apartment, with her boring nine-to-five job and her lonely existence. At least she knew she wouldn't have to deal with stupid men who were so arrogant their heads were buried up their own asses.

* * * *

"I told you Vanessa was a bitch, Gage. I knew April didn't have it in her to be mean for no reason. And as far I am concerned, she wasn't being mean, she was defending herself. If that bitch had spat in my face, I would have killed her, and so would have you," Saxon said.

"Shit. I've really fucked up, haven't I? What the hell are we going to do now?" Gage asked with frustration. He was really angry at himself for jumping to conclusions where Vanessa and April were concerned. Gage had always known what a conniving bitch Vanessa was. He hadn't stopped to think at all. He had taken one look at his mate standing over Vanessa, with the bitch's hair wrapped around her wrist, taken a look at Vanessa's fearful face, and acted. He had let his previous bedding of the bitch, as well as her contrived innocent expression, rule him.

Gage indicated for his seasoned warriors to go after their mate and lead her back to the palace. If she kept walking the way she was, she would end up in the middle of the lion clan's pride. That was the last thing he wanted to happen, after Leo had been eying their mate as if she belonged to him. He watched as his warriors led April past them and she didn't even glance his way. His warriors had surrounded her with their bodies, making sure she was protected from any danger as they led her back home.

* * * *

April couldn't believe the change in the disposition of Gage and Saxon's warriors. One moment they had been scowling at her as if she were an inconvenience, the next they were introducing themselves, being so courteous and solicitous, it was laughable. She had no idea what had made their demeanor change toward her, but she wasn't about to look a gift horse in the mouth. She knew she wasn't going to remember all their names, but she actually felt she was being accepted for who she was for the first time in her life. Maybe they had liked the way she stood up to her mates, and instead of frowning at her as they had been, now they were smiling and surrounding her to protect her.

April vowed she was going to befriend these kind warriors and totally ignore her own mates. They were going to have to do some big-time groveling before she would let them back into her good graces. She had been really hurt when Gage had immediately thought the scuffle between her and Vanessa was all her fault. She had been defending herself and not instigating the fight as Gage had believed, and it hurt her to be on the end of his anger without him asking her side of the story. She pushed those thoughts aside when one of Gage and Saxon's seasoned warriors called her name, bringing her out of her speculation.

April was kept occupied by the warriors as they made their way back to the palace. It was dark by the time they arrived, and she was surprised to find herself in a great banquet hall. There were people everywhere, and she was feeling hurt and angry. She wondered why her mates hadn't brought her to the dining hall before, instead of leaving it to their warriors to do so for the first time. Two of the warriors escorted April to a long table on a raised dais at the front of the room. She thanked the warriors she thought were named Tam and Stephan and asked them to join her at the large table. She didn't want to be the only person sitting under the gaze of the curious people here. The two men sat down at the table, leaving gaps between them. She assumed the empty chairs were intended for her so-called mates. She felt very uncomfortable being under the scrutiny of so many people and couldn't help but wish her mates would hurry up and arrive. No sooner had that thought entered her head than her three mates entered the dining banquet room. All noise ceased as Gage, Saxon, and Ben took their places, standing behind the empty chairs on the raised dais.

April kept her head bent down, her eyes firmly fixed on the pristine white tablecloth in front of her. She hoped the people's eyes were now diverted to her mates rather than herself. The crowd of people below began to fidget as the silence stretched on. April raised her head and looked from Gage to Saxon then Ben. They were standing still, staring out over the crowd, watching the doors on the far side of the room. A commotion could be heard from behind the closed doors, which drew all eyes toward them. The doors were pushed open so hard they slammed against the wall behind them. There were three tall, strong warriors entering the room. The first one had his hands free, and April realized he must have been the one to open the double doors with such force. The other two tall, brawny warriors were pulling a beautiful, screaming shrew along with them as they entered.

April couldn't believe the filth coming out of Vanessa's mouth. She would have put a sailor to shame. She screamed at the warriors, but they seemed to be totally oblivious to her fury. They dragged her kicking and screaming until they were mere feet away from the raised table. Then to Vanessa's humiliation and April's shock, they stripped the woman until she was naked in front of the entire congregation and pushed her down onto her knees. Vanessa must have realized the futility of her struggles and finally gave up trying to escape. Vanessa raised her head to look at April, giving her a look so full of hate and maliciousness it shocked her. April tried to keep her expression blank, hoping she looked far more serene than she actually felt.

April watched Gage walk along the dais to the end, step down, and move around to stand a foot away from the furious woman. He totally ignored her as he stared into the crowded room.

"This woman has disrespected our mate by coming into our bedchamber, maligning her position in our household, and then spitting in her face. She has just been stripped of all her possessions and will be stripped of her position in this clan. She is to be banished as soon as I have finished speaking. It is also my shame that I castigated my mate when she defended herself against this bitch," Gage stated to the crowd.

April couldn't believe what she had just heard. She had to bite her tongue to keep her gasp of surprise contained as Gage turned his back on the woman at his feet and then proceeded to kneel in supplication to her.

"April, I give you my humblest apologies at the way you have been treated in this house. I hope you will find it within your heart to forgive a fool of a man blind to the sly, vicious wiles of the insignificant woman behind me," Gage stated, then bowed his head to her.

April was too surprised, then humbled, as her proud warrior subjugated himself to her. She felt a lump of emotion clogging her chest, making it impossible to reply, so she bowed her head to Gage with acceptance. April watched as Gage released a sigh then rose to his feet and headed back to the steps at the end of the dais.

April watched as Saxon walked down the steps and stood in front of the humiliated Vanessa. He stood side-on to the table, and she saw him look out over the crowd, ignoring the woman at his feet. Then he slowly looked down at her upturned face, and even April blanched at the fury on his face.

"Vanessa, you have been stripped of your clothes and also your position within the panther clan. You are banished for the rest of your life. If you are found on panther-clan land, you will be killed. If you come near our mate or try to harm her in any way, I will personally rip your head from your fucking shoulders," Saxon roared at the woman cowering at his feet. April saw him turn to the two warriors a little behind and to the sides of the horrible woman. "Make sure you escort this woman from panther land. Take some of the young warriors with you. Maybe they will also learn from this incident on how to keep track of a woman."

April couldn't believe they were banishing Vanessa from their clan. The woman had more right to be here than she did. Maybe she could plead with Saxon to stop the punishment they had chosen for the jealous woman. April stood up and quickly walked to the opposite end of the raised table, down the two steps, and over toward Saxon. As she moved, she saw Vanessa pull one of her arms out of the grip of the warrior holding it. April saw a flash of silver just before Vanessa turned and flung something at Saxon. April didn't even think about what she was doing. She was already moving quickly and leapt the last couple of feet in front of her mate. She gave a gasp as she felt pain radiate from her shoulder, across her back, and down her arm. She stumbled, her knees feeling weak all of a sudden, and knew she was going to disgrace herself by falling flat on her face.

April covered her ears as Saxon let out a roar full of anguish and anger as he caught her in his arms. April whimpered at the sight of a silver knife protruding from her shoulder and felt sick to her stomach. Saxon gently took her down to the floor with him and cradled her over his lap, on her side, as he stared down at her.

* * * *

Gage leapt across the room at Vanessa then knocked her down. He was still so furious he wanted to pick her up and knock her down again. He had never done anything like that before in his life. He ordered his warriors to remove Vanessa from his presence and lock her in the dungeon below. He turned and stared in anguish at the knife stuck in his mate's shoulder and the blood running from the wound.

Gage saw Ben was at Saxon and April's side. He bellowed for their healer, which was totally unnecessary as he was already in the room and had witnessed the incident.

Gage realized April had fainted and was thankful as the healer quickly pulled the knife from her shoulder. He grabbed a tablecloth from a nearby table, ripped it into strips, and handed it over to the healer, and the man began to bind the wound tightly, trying to stem the flow of blood.

"Saxon, we need to get your mate to bed, so I may tend her wound. Please, Sire, pick your mate up and carry her to your bedchamber," the healer demanded of his Alpha. Gage heard the healer give a sigh of relief as his friend, Ben, took his mate from Saxon and carried her from the room. Gage followed Ben and knew his brother and the healer were close at his heels.

Chapter Seven

April raged with fever over the next several days. The healer had done all he could to stop infection from setting into her wound. He had cleaned her shoulder with pure alcohol then added a poultice of herbs over the stitching holding her wound together and wrapped it with strips of cloth. One of her mates stayed with her at all times. Saxon vowed to not leave her alone at all until she was fully recovered, as she had taken the blade meant for him. He felt guilty, because he knew the knife blade would never have reached its mark. He was able to move a hell of a lot faster than his small mate had, but he had not seen her coming toward him. He had kept his eyes on the vicious bitch being led from the room. Even though he had seen her pull her arm from one of the guards, he was chiding himself for not seeing her pick up the knife.

Ben was just as determined as he was not to leave their mate. Since Saxon was riddled with guilt, he demanded that Ben leave him to care for their mate. The two ended up scuffling around the floor of the bedchamber, which is where Gage found them. Gage walked over to him and Ben, grabbed them by their shoulders, and pulled them apart. Saxon turned to see April watching them from the bed. She was sitting up against a mound of pillows, her eyes glazed with fever and her skin flushed red. He saw her push the covers aside, and she was on her feet before he could stop her. She stood naked before him, swaying on her feet as she stared at them. Saxon, his brother, and Ben rushed over to her side but halted when she began to speak.

"How could you do this to me? You've taken me away from the only best friend I have. You've made choices without asking me if I wanted what you've decided. You've treated me like I was a criminal, when I was only defending myself. I want to go home," April wailed. She was obviously out of her mind with pain and fever. She probably had no idea she was shouting every word. Saxon reached for her and gently picked her up. He set her back on the bed, but didn't leave her side. She was so hot to touch, she practically burned his hands.

April was delirious with her fever and her rantings each day and night. But what hurt Saxon most of all was when she yelled she didn't belong in their world and wanted to go home. He knew it was their fault she didn't feel liked she belonged. He was going to do his best to make sure she felt differently from now on. She was the most precious thing to him, and he loved her more than his own life.

* * * *

April's fever finally broke on the fifth night after her injury. She woke up to find an elderly man leaning over her shoulder, inspecting her wound. She gave a small start and tried to move away from the man. He soothed her fear with his deep, melodious voice.

"It's all right, April. I am only inspecting your wound. I should be able to take the stitches out of your shoulder in a couple of days. How are you feeling?"

"Like I've been hit by a truck," she answered, then wondered why her throat was so sore. "What's your name? I've never met you before, have I?"

"Well, not officially, no. My name is Reece. I am the clan healer. I have been taking care of your injury. You've been quite ill. It's no surprise you're feeling ragged."

"Thanks for looking after me. I really would like to take a bath. I feel like something the cat dragged in," April muttered.

Reece looked appalled at her statement, which made April wonder what she had said to upset the man. When she realized what she had said and what type of shifters she was living with, she couldn't contain herself. She burst out laughing. She laughed harder at the sight of Reece's shocked expression, until she had tears pouring down her face. She finally exhausted herself and was too tired to laugh anymore. She was feeling as weak as a kitten. She didn't stop smiling, though. Reece left the room, giving her a look over his shoulder. He smiled and winked at her, and she knew the healer had only pretended to be appalled by her statement and humor.

April waited until Reece had closed the door behind him and flung the covers away from her. She swung her legs over the side of the bed then sat waiting for the dizziness to pass and her strength to return. Once she was able, she slowly walked toward the bathroom, sat down on the side of the large bathing pool, and slid down the step until she was surrounded by the warm, fragrant water. She swam over to the other side of the pool, grabbed some shampoo, and washed her hair. Then she started on her body. When she finished, she was so tired she barely had the strength to lift her arms. She knew she had to get out and dry herself off, but didn't know if she would be able to find the energy.

She had just made it to the steps leading out of the pool as Ben walked in. She looked at him then quickly looked away again. She wanted him to leave her alone so she could dry off and get back into bed, but she knew she was going to need his help.

"What are you doing out of bed, April? You shouldn't be taking a bath by yourself," Ben said firmly.

April didn't respond. She just looked away with frustration. She really did need help, but was not going to ask Ben for it. She stubbornly stood, swaying on her feet as she dried herself then headed back into the bedroom. April didn't quite make it. She was mere feet from the bed when her knees gave out. Her legs buckled beneath her body. She hadn't heard Ben come up behind her, but she was thankful she didn't land on the cold, hard marble floor. He scooped her up into his arms and laid her down on the bed, covered her with the blankets and comforter, then kissed her cheek and left the room.

April felt much better the next day. Most of her strength had returned, so after she bathed and dressed, she began to wander throughout the palatial mansion. She hadn't had enough time or much of an interest to get her bearings when she had first been forced to come to her new home. She had finally resigned herself to the fact she would probably never be able to get back to her own home, and to be honest with herself, she wasn't sure if she really wanted to. Besides Olivia, there was nothing for her to get back home for. She just didn't know if there was anything for her to make her want to stay here either.

April wandered the palace and the grounds until she knew where everything was. All the while, she was followed around by at least two of the seasoned warriors. She had first thought they were assigned to her to protect her, but her self-confidence had waned since she had arrived in this strange new land, and she was beginning to wonder if the guards were assigned to protect others from her, especially after the incident with Vanessa.

Over the next few days, April only seemed to see her supposed mates at meal times in the large banquet dining room. She had no idea why they seemed so distant with her. She had taken to sitting away from them at the back of one of the lower tables, and when they didn't try to demand she sit up on the raised dais with them, she knew then they didn't care what she did. As much as it broke her heart, April made up her mind to try and find her way home. She felt like she had no friends in this place and was really missing Olivia. She was sick and tired of being treated like a leper. April began to lose weight rapidly as she picked at her meals without really consuming any food. She spent more and more of her time in the garden, ignoring everyone and everything. She spent most of her time sitting in the shade on the bench near the large fish pond, staring into space.

One night when the evening meal was over and her mates were sitting at the head table deep in discussion, April left the room. She couldn't bear to see them, to be in the same room as them and not have them touch her or be able to touch them in return. She missed the feel of their arms around her. She missed her cuddles with Ben, her conversations with Saxon, and believe it or not, she even missed butting heads with Gage.

* * * *

Gage, Saxon, and Ben began to plan to woo their mate back to them. They had been giving April her space lately, but Gage didn't want to lose the one and only woman he loved from the bad decisions and actions he had made. Even though he had apologized, Gage still knew he was the one fully responsible for the dissension between the three of them and April, but he had no idea how to go about making things right between them.

Gage, Saxon, and Ben followed April into the gardens the following morning after their breakfast. They kept their distance from her until she had settled herself down onto the bench in the shade, and then they approached her. Gage came at her from one side, indicated to Saxon to come from the other side, and told Ben to take an arc on the other side of the garden, blocking her in from the front He didn't want his mate to have a chance to leave before he spoke to her. Gage took a seat beside April, took her hand in his own, and began to make light circles on the sensitive skin of her inner wrist. He was heartened when she didn't immediately pull away from him. He began speaking to her in a calm, quiet voice.

"I know my apology can never make up for my actions toward you, but I would like to, again, apologize for the way I have treated you. I knew what Vanessa was like, and I know I jumped to conclusions when I saw you defending yourself from that she-bitch. I would turn the clock back and change what I said to you if I could. Please, will you give me, Saxon, and Ben another chance? If you are willing to let Saxon and Ben back into your life and you can't find it in your heart to forgive me, I will understand. It is me you should be directing your anger to, not Saxon, and especially not Ben. Ben has done nothing to you that you have not let him. He asked you if he could claim you before he did so. He gave you a choice, April, not like me, when I commanded Saxon to claim you the same way I did. Please don't hate me, April. You have to realize there is only ever one mate for our kind. We thought we would never have the chance to mate with a female. When we found you asleep in the forest, I caught your scent and knew right away you were Saxon's and my mate. I think I went a little crazy. I didn't want you to have the chance to leave us before we got to know you. I know it's hard for you to comprehend what I am trying to explain, because you aren't a shifter. But bear in mind, we are also half animal, and it is natural for an animal to want to claim their mate as soon as they find her. I only want you to be happy, April," Gage finished. He raised April's hand to his mouth, kissed her knuckles, placed her hand back in her lap, and left.

Gage watched from the cover of the bushes as Saxon moved in and took the place he had just vacated. Saxon took April's had in his own and sat quietly, just holding her hand. Gage could hear her elevated breathing and then heard her trying to stifle a sniffle. His brother moved his other hand beneath April's chin, gently raised her face to his, and stared into her moisture-filled eyes. Gage's heart was aching as he watched his mate cry silently beside his brother.

"I love you, April, and so does Gage. He is an Alpha male just like I am, but his communication skills suck. We have the responsibility of the entire panther clan to contend with before our own. We are not infallible, we do make mistakes. After all, we are part human. I'm sure we will make mistakes in the future, as well, just as you will. Will you want us to hold a grudge against you when you have erred? Would you want us to not forgive you for being human? Please give us another chance. We want you to be happy and healthy. We want to see that spark of fire return to your eyes when you look at us. I know if you asked him to help you find your way back home, Gage would help you. He loves you so much he would be willing to let you go if that is what you want. I love you, too. It would break my heart if you left us, but if that is what you truly wish, what your heart truly desires, then we will do our damnedest to make it happen. Please, will you give us another chance?" Saxon asked. He leaned down, placed a kiss on her forehead, stood, and left.

* * * *

Ben took Saxon's place on the bench, but instead of taking hold of his mate's hand as his friends had, he scooped her up into his lap and cradled her against chest. He didn't speak at all, just relished having her back in his arms.

He just held her, offering her the comfort he knew she desperately needed. It didn't take long for the dam to break. Ben pulled April tightly against him and rocked back and forth as she sobbed out all her hurt. Ben knew April was one of those people who turned silent and kept her distance when she had been hurt. He wondered if she had ever had anyone to lean on, to help her and listen to her when she needed comfort. He had seen the pain in her eyes and knew she had tried to lock her emotions away so she couldn't be hurt again. He was the only one who knew how deeply Gage had wounded his mate when he had berated her for defending herself. His lack of trust was what had hurt her the most. He knew there was still a long way to go before they really knew each other. He only hoped April would give them the opportunity to do so. The storm eventually petered out, but April didn't try to move away from him, and he was content just to feel her in his arms once more. He knew her heart was big enough to love all three of them, if she would just trust herself. She was fighting herself more that she was fighting the three of them. She obviously lacked confidence in her own decisions and didn't trust her own heart. He wondered who had hurt her so much to make her doubt herself. He would like nothing better than to find the bastard and rip his heart from his chest. April needed time to learn the value of her own self-worth. He, Gage, and Saxon had to find a way to show her how valuable she really was to them, and then maybe she would begin to believe it herself and trust her own heart. He looked down into her relaxed face. She had totally exhausted herself with her fit of tears. It didn't bother him, though. He wanted to keep a hold of her for as long as he could.

Chapter Eight

April seemed more like her old self after she had cried a storm over Ben's chest, drenching his hard pectorals with her salty tears. She had known the storm would break eventually. She was one of those people who bottled everything up until all of a sudden the walls would crumble. She hated the way she was, but she could do nothing about it. She had learned to keep everything to herself. She'd never had any brothers or sisters growing up. Her parents had been too self-absorbed with their own lives to worry about their own daughter's well-being. They had been more concerned about keeping up the appearance they thought was required of them by their elite neighbors.

April could have told them those snobby people weren't worth it, but she didn't want to waste her breath. Nothing she said had ever been acknowledged by her parents. They were too busy spending money like it was going out of style, renovating a house that didn't need a makeover, and changing from one expensive car to another, just to be like their medical-professional and socialite neighbors. Little did April know, they had gone through her mother's inheritance and were in dire straits financially.

Everything had come out when her father had killed her mother and then turned the gun on himself. She had learned her true self-worth then. Her parents' message to her had been that money and lifestyle were way more important than their own flesh and blood. It had taken months for her parents' lawyers to wade through the bills accumulated by her parents' lavishness. April had been happy not having to pay back a debt from her parents' lack of discipline and had been able to start her life over. In the end, everything her parents owned had just covered the cost of all the bills, giving April room to breathe and finally start a life of her own, unencumbered by her parents' debt. She had picked herself up, dusted herself off, and worked her way through college, ending up with a degree in English. When she had finished college, she had been lucky enough to land the first job she had applied for, working for a small publishing company. She had a small, cheap, run-down apartment, but to her it was a mansion. She had earned the money herself and didn't have to answer to anyone or hide her true feelings. She had finally been able to be herself. Everything had changed again the last night she had said good-bye to Olivia. Her self-worth was yet again taking a beating. She had wondered if she would ever fit in and be accepted for who she really was.

April knew she had a temper. Her anger was always slow to be ignited, but when it was, whoever was around her had better get out of the way. Olivia was the only person who had ever accepted April for who she was. Now it seemed Ben understood her more than she understood herself. He'd held her when she needed it most and let her cry out her pain and frustration. She hadn't even realized that was what she had needed until she was in his arms sobbing her heart out. He seemed to be more in tune to her emotions than she was. She wondered how she had gotten so lost and lacked trust to accept her own intuition.

Once April was done with her self-pity party, her brain began to process all her mates had told her. Saxon had said he and Gage loved her. She had believed Saxon. She could see the emotion in his eyes when he had declared his love for her, and she knew with her whole being that Ben loved her as much as she loved him. She had feelings for Saxon. Who wouldn't? He, Gage, and Ben were all the epitome of Alpha males with the faces of Adonis and the bodies of Hercules. She was still uncertain where she stood with Gage, though. He was such an arrogant, dominant male, she wondered if they would ever get along or if they would always be wary of each other and end up at each other's throats.

All she'd ever wanted was to be loved and accepted for who she was. Was Gage even capable of giving her that? She had no idea. She knew she should give him another chance. She knew she had made mistakes over her short lifetime and that the only way for anyone to learn was from making their own mistakes and then trying to make up for their transgressions, to right wrongs the best way they could and ask for forgiveness. She knew deep down she loved all her mates equally and she was going to forgive Gage.

April sighed as she entered the large dining banquet room. Instead of taking her usual seat at the back of the room, she headed for the raised dais and took her seat between Ben and Gage. She became aware of eyes focusing on her and the noise in the room diminishing to a low level. The clan members assigned to the duty of feeding everyone began to bring in platters of food. They started with their table and then moved to the back of the room until every table had platters of food along the middle of it. April wondered why they were always served first instead of the clan members. Saxon had said it was Gage's and his job to look after the clan, and April thought the other clan members should be served first, as they were the ones that kept the palatial household running efficiently, but she was too timid to make her thoughts known.

It wasn't until the words Gage had stated to her earlier that morning popped into her brain that she found a little of her famous backbone. *"I want you to be happy, April."*

April turned to Gage and looked into his face. The sight of his handsome face, sexy eyes, and the muscles rippling beneath his skin as he moved took her breath away. She looked into his eyes and saw the heat in them for her as he looked back at her. She cleared her throat so she wouldn't squeak when she began to talk.

"I was wondering why we are served food first when the reason there is food on the table for us to eat is a result of the members of the clan. Wouldn't it be prudent to serve your people first and serve yourself last, to show them you appreciate all the hard work and effort they put in for each meal we eat?" April asked.

The smile was slow to emerge across Gage's face, but when it did, it took April's breath away. He looked at her with such hunger, she squirmed in her seat to try and relieve the ache that began throbbing in her pussy. She lowered her eyes to the tablecloth, hoping Gage hadn't seen the reaction in her eyes. Gage surprised April yet again. He stood to his feet and waited until the room became quiet. All eyes were turned his way as he began to address the members of his clan.

"I have yet again another reason to apologize. This time to you, the members of our clan." Gage paused as he took April's hand in his own and gently pulled her to her feet to stand beside him. "My mate, April, your Alpha female, has pointed out to me the amount of work everyone in this clan does to keep my household running smoothly. From now on, you will be served the food first in appreciation for the diligent hard work you all put in as members of this clan. You have my gratitude, as well as that of my brother's and Ben's from the bear clan. But most of all, you have earned the respect and gratitude of your Alpha female, April. It was her suggestion to have the head table served last. From now on, the law is to serve yourselves first and your Alphas last."

April couldn't believe what Gage had just done on her behalf. He had listened to her suggestion and then acted on it immediately. The cheering of the crowd diminished as she stood looking at Gage in shock. She could feel herself being pulled into his eyes and never wanted to let go. She felt worthy again, for the first time in such a long time she didn't know how to deal with it. She pulled her hand away from Gage and ran to the side doors and out into the garden. Tears pricked the back of her eyes. Happiness, love, and joy created a huge lump in her chest, and she tried to swallow and breathe around it without breaking down and bawling like a baby. Her chest and throat were so tight she thought she'd never be able to get enough air into her lungs. She found herself in her usual place, sitting on the bench seat near the fish pond. She breathed in the clean, humid air until the tight constriction left her chest and throat. She didn't hear Gage following her until he sat down next to her and pulled her up onto his lap. April didn't fight him. She was so tired of fighting to keep her emotions locked away. So instead she snuggled into his chest, wrapped her arms around his waist, and held him tight.

* * * *

"You have earned the respect and appreciation of my clan, April. You are the most selfless person I have ever met. You make me feel ashamed of the selfishness in which I have acted. You are such a beautiful person inside and out. I don't ever want to lose you. You have earned my respect and gratitude far more than any other person in this clan, including my own brother. I need you to keep my head from getting too large. Please, give me another chance, baby. I can't tell you how sorry I am for the way I treated you." Gage pulled away from April so he could see her face. He could see the hunger behind her eyes as she stared up at him.

"I accept your apology. I, too, should be apologizing to you. I have learned over the years to keep my emotions locked away. I need to learn to communicate with you so my problems, fears, and hurt don't compound until they explode out of me. You will need to be patient with me, as it will take a long time to undo the behavior I have had drummed into me since I was a small child. So, I, too, am sorry for the way I treated you," April finished in a quiet voice.

Gage stared down into April's eyes and was humbled by his mate's acceptance of his faults as well as her own. He leaned down and brushed his lips over hers. He only meant to give her a quick peck on the lips then lead her back into the banquet dining hall to eat. But the first taste of her after such a long drought was like trying to quench a massive thirst with a sip of water instead of the whole glass.

Gage deepened the kiss. He slanted his mouth over hers again and again, thrusting his tongue into the depths of her moist cavern, his tongue dueling with her own. He growled low in his throat as his blood heated and set his body on fire. His hands began to roam over the curves of her body as he devoured her mouth.

Gage slid his hand beneath the hem of April's short skirt, slowly inching his hand higher and higher. He withdrew his mouth from hers, staring into her eyes as he moved his hand the final few inches until he was cupping her hot, wet mound. The feel of her cream-dewed lips heated his blood even more, and he knew he needed to touch her, to bring her pleasure with his fingers. Otherwise he would fuck her in the garden, not caring if they were caught or not. He wanted to see her face turn slack with passion, to hear her moan as he pleasured her body. He wanted to give without taking for the first time in his life.

Gage slid his fingers through the slick folds of April's sex, coating the tips of two fingers with her pussy juice, then worked his way up to the top of her slit. He slowly began to massage the little nub of sensitive nerves protruding at the top of her pussy with whisper-soft touches. When April thrust her hips up into his hand, he applied a little more pressure, making his fingers dance over her flesh. He leaned down, covering her lips with his own, taking her cries of passion into his own mouth. He ravaged her mouth as he fondled her cunt, the sound of her crying out with unrestrained delight as he pleasured her music to his ears. He moved his fingers back down to her hole and thrust them up into her tight, wet sheath. He pumped his fingers in and out of her pussy, over and over again, then placed his thumb over her clit, tapping it firmly. He held her body to his as April screamed into his mouth, her hips pumping up and down on his embedded fingers as she convulsed and pulsed, clamping down hard on his digits. He enhanced her pleasure, kept his fingers pumping until the last flutter of her muscles ceased. He finally withdrew his coated fingers and hand then lapped up every single drop of her cum. He couldn't help his animal instincts and knew his mate could hear him purring as he lapped up the last of her cream.

Gage stood to his feet, taking April with him, cradling her against his chest as he hurried from the gardens, heading for their bedchamber.

Saxon, find Ben and come to the bedchamber. Now. We need to pleasure our mate, Gage stated telepathically as he practically ran through the palace hallways.

Are you sure this is what April wants? Have you asked her? Or have you taken over again and, in your normal arrogance, assumed this is what she wants? Saxon asked.

Saxon's question made Gage pause mid stride. He was a few feet away from the door to the bedchamber. He looked down into April's upturned face. The hunger for him was evident in her eyes, but she had also raised a brow quizzically. He wasn't sure if the raised brow was to question his cease of movement, or the fact he was railroading her so he could release his own desires with his mate. Gage opened the door to the bedchamber, strode directly to the bed, and lowered April to sit on the side. He knelt down in front of her and took both her hands into his own.

"April, we want to make love with you. Saxon and Ben are waiting to see if that is what you want, as well. We want to pleasure you all night long, baby, but if you're not ready, please tell me now. If I go any further, I don't think I'll be able to control myself. My panther is pushing at me to take you. I would never hurt you, April, but I need you more than you'll ever know," Gage stated, letting the love he felt for his mate shine from his eyes.

"You scared me, Gage. I want to know you won't change into your panther form like you did to me when I first arrived. Please, don't ever to that to me again. Not unless I ask you to," April said vehemently.

"I promise, baby. I'm so sorry I scared you. That was not my intention. My beast took over, wanted to mark and claim you as my own. I am more in control now that we have mated once before. My beast won't wrestle that control away from me again," Gage replied, sincerity in his voice.

He heard April take a deep breath as she looked into his eyes. He felt joy surge through him as she looked back at him, letting him see the love she felt for him as he let him see the love he felt for her.

"I want you to answer me, baby. I will not touch you intimately again until you tell me it's what you want, too."

"Yes, Gage. I want you, Saxon, and Ben to make love to me, pleasure me all night long," April replied, with a smile full of love on her face, then launched herself from the side of the bed, down into his lap.

April grabbed two handfuls of Gage's hair and brought his head down to meet hers. She opened her mouth slightly and began to kiss his lips. Gage took over the kiss. He devoured her mouth as he gave his brother the answer to his long-awaited questions.

It's what she wants. Come now.

Chapter Nine

Saxon ran through the hallways of the palace with Ben at his side, not stopping to speak to anyone until he had the bedchamber doors within sight. He stopped and took deep breaths, letting them out slowly as he pushed his raging libido back down, getting control of himself. He saw Ben was in the same condition as he was and knew the last thing he wanted to do was scare his mate with his own eagerness. Ben opened the doors, and Saxon stepped through the doorway, closing them quickly behind them. He sought and found April and Gage on the floor beside the bed, kissing each other passionately. April was straddling Gage's lap, rocking her hips back and forth over Gage's hard cock through the fabric of his pants. Gage eased his mouth away from April's and stood to his feet in a graceful, fluid motion, taking her with him. He set her down on the side of the bed, stepped back from her, and began to remove his clothes. Saxon moved farther into the room with Ben at his side.

Saxon stalked toward April, keeping his heated eyes on her, as he and Ben stripped their pants and boots from their bodies. Saxon stood in front of her naked and aroused, without any discomfort or vulnerability, his friends at his side. He stood proudly with his shoulders back, his legs braced shoulder width apart, his hips tilted toward her, drawing April's eyes to his bobbing erection.

* * * *

April had a hard time believing she'd had their cocks in her body without being torn apart. They all had massive erections, but they differed, as well. Gage's cock was thicker than Ben's and Saxon's. Saxon's was longer than Ben's and Gage's, and Ben's cock was nearly as thick as Gage's but tilted up at the end. It looked like his cock had been made specifically to pleasure a woman's G-spot. April didn't know if she made a noise to break their concentration as they stood staring at her with hungry eyes, but all of a sudden they moved as one.

Gage reached her first, pulling her up to her feet. He grabbed the hem of the small skirt she was wearing and tore it from her body. Ben grabbed at the top covering her breasts and ripped it in half. April felt feminine but also vulnerable, standing with the three men eying her exposed body. She moved her arms up and began to cover her breasts with her hands, only to have them pulled back down to her sides then behind her back.

Saxon was now standing behind her, clasping her wrists in one of his large hands, holding her captive. She felt her pussy throb and contract with need as she was held prisoner. Ben proceeded to rip the arm holes of her top until it fell from her body in pieces. The only thing she had left on were the soft boots covering her feet and calves.

Saxon released her hands as Gage picked her up. He placed her in the middle of the large bed and stared at her, communicating with her, telling her not to move from where he had placed her. The three men walked away from her, heading toward the big carved timber doors. April had to bite her tongue to stop herself from crying out. She wanted to beg them not to leave her, to make love to her, but knew she wouldn't. She had never begged anyone for anything in her life, except when she begged them to let her go home, and she wasn't about to beg these men to love her. She felt tears prick behind her eyes. Closing her eyelids, she prayed for the strength to hold the tears at bay. She didn't want them to know how much they were hurting her by walking away.

April heard a drawer open then close. She didn't open her eyes, thinking they were getting clean clothes and then would be leaving her alone again. She should be used to being lonely. After all, she only had one true friend. She didn't want to be left alone again. She felt pain pierce her heart, and the tears she'd been trying to hold back began to leak from the corner of her eyes. She didn't hear them come back to her, but she felt the bed dip as three very large men crawled onto it. She opened her eyes to see them watching her, frowns marring their faces as they watched her struggle to compose herself.

Ben moved in closer to her, reached out his arms, and scooped her up until she was sitting on his lap. April could feel his cock pulsing against her hip, the wet tip leaving pre-cum on her heated skin.

"Why are you crying, honey? What's the matter?" Ben asked with concern.

April was too choked up with emotion, the large lump in her chest and the tightness in her throat making her mute. She shook her head and leaned against his warm, hard chest, breathing deeply, trying to regain control of her emotions.

"April, baby. What's wrong?" Saxon asked as he sat down on the bed next to her and Ben.

Again, April just shook her head, keeping her eyes closed, tears flowing over her cheeks to drip onto Ben's chest.

Gage scooped April up from Ben and placed her on the mattress. He pulled her arms up above her head, quickly wrapping her wrists with soft yet strong material, and tied her to the headboard. She hadn't even had a chance to blink. He moved back down the bed until he was lying beside her and stared into her eyes.

"What are you doing? Why have you tied me up? Let me go," April cried out, tugging against the soft restraints binding her.

"Ben and Saxon asked you a question. You will answer them," Gage commanded, his voice laced with steel.

April closed her mouth stubbornly and closed her eyes again. She turned her head away from Gage, unequivocally trying to ignore the three men. She felt Gage move away from her but was too afraid to open her eyes. She didn't want to watch him leave the room in disgust. She opened her eyes again on a gasp as she felt two hands move up her inner thighs, stroking her skin and parting her legs at the same time. Gage was sitting between her splayed thighs, staring at her pussy with such hunger it made her breath catch.

"You will answer us in the end, April. Why not save yourself the torture of trying to fight us?" Gage asked.

April moaned and arched her hips up with delight at the first lick of a warm, wet, raspy tongue on her pussy. She opened her eyes to see Gage's head bent to her pussy, his eyes watching her as he once more licked her cunt from top to bottom. She saw the glint of satisfaction in his eyes as she whimpered at the pleasure he was lavishing on her. Then she knew, with certainty, they would never hurt her. They had told her they loved her. They weren't going to inflict her with pain. They were going to torture her with pleasure.

April saw Ben and Saxon move in her peripheral vision as Gage began to lick her pussy in earnest. Ben and Saxon moved to either side of her body, took a breast each in their large hands, bent their heads, and began to suck her nipples. The feel of the rhythmic pulling on her sensitive nipples and Gage's raspy, feline tongue licking her cunt had her on the edge of orgasm within moments. April was aware of her body's acceptance as they bestowed her with pleasure by the way she was arching up into their mouths. All of a sudden, the three men pulled away from her, leaving her hanging on the edge of ecstasy. April sobbed out her frustration at being left hanging.

"What are you doing to me? Why did you stop?"

"I told you we would torture the answer from you. Now answer the question, April. Why were you upset?" Gage asked again. He stared at her as he waited for her answer.

* * * *

Gage growled with frustration as their mate once again closed her eyes and pulled her lips together in a straight, thin line. He bent his head back down, gently grasped hold of her engorged clit between his teeth, and began to flick his tongue over the sensitive nub. He had to move one of his hands onto her lower abdomen to hold her hips in place while he pleasured her with his mouth. She was wriggling and bucking around so much, he was in danger of being bucked away from his delectable snack. The fingers of his splayed hand over her stomach gently massaged her skin, placing pressure over her womb and pubic bone. He moved his mouth off her clit, licking his way down between her folds until he was at her dripping, creaming vagina. He moved his free hand up to the top of her slit and pulled her flesh taut, sliding the protective hood back and exposing her engorged pearl of flesh. He gently massaged the little nub with the pad of his finger then stabbed his tongue into her juicy, cream-filled hole. He groaned as her cream coated his tongue, her muscles clamping around his penetrating muscle, her pussy trying to draw more of him into her body. Gage pulled away again when he felt her flutter on his tongue. He had brought her to the edge once more with the help of his brother and Ben.

"Why were you upset, honey?" Ben asked. Gage was pleased when his friend began to question April. He seemed to be able to converse with April on a deeper level, and Gage knew if she was going to answer one of them, it would most likely be him. Gage knew April thought Ben the less dominant of her mates, but little did she know, he was probably more dominant than Gage himself. His friend just knew how to get around women better than he and his brother did. Ben had grown up with sisters and had a fair understanding of how the female mind worked.

"I didn't want you to leave me." April sobbed. Gage watched as she rocked her hips, no doubt trying to relieve the ache deep in her body.

"Why did you think we were leaving, April?" Saxon asked this time.

"You turned away from me. Everyone always leaves me." Gage

watched as his brother took April's face between his large hands and stared down into their mate's pain-filled eyes.

"We weren't leaving you, baby. We were just getting some toys to play with. We want your body so consumed with pleasure, you can't see straight. We are dominant men, April. We like to take control in the bedroom. Your pleasure is our pleasure. Why would you think we would strip you naked, place you on the bed, and then leave you and ourselves unfulfilled?"

Gage watched April stare at Saxon as she processed what his brother said to her. They hadn't been leaving her.

"Answer the question, April," Gage demanded.

"My father killed my mother then killed himself. Their precious money, or lack of it, was more important to them than I was. They left me alone to fend for myself, not that that was much different to when they were alive. You see, I cramped their style. I was an accident that was never supposed to happen. My parents were more interested in keeping up with the elite neighbors than they were about me, their child. I once heard my mother telling one of her so-called friends if she had found out she was pregnant earlier and wouldn't have had to put her own life at risk, she would have aborted me. I was just making them spend their money on unnecessary items such as clothes and food. If it wasn't for me, maybe they wouldn't have had to spend anything on me and would have never ended up broke. My father couldn't stand the thought of the neighbors finding out that he was ruined financially. I meant nothing to them. The money they had and lost was more important to them than their own daughter," April reiterated, no emotion in her voice as she recited her story by rote.

Gage felt pain stab at his heart. He knew Saxon and Ben felt their mate's pain, as well. She had told them how her parents, her flesh and blood, had treated her without any emotion whatsoever, but he could see the pain to the depths of her soul. His mate had never had the love of another human being. She kept part of herself hidden away, even from herself. He could see the compassion she had for others. She had shown it with her actions already. His mate was so fragile. Gage was afraid that one more false move, one more indelicate statement of arrogance from him, would break her. Gage wasn't sure whether to continue to make love to April, or to pull her into his arms and cuddle her. He was about to ask Saxon and Ben what they thought when his little, fragile mate came apart.

The first sob caught him off guard as much as it had April. He could tell by the shocked look on her face. The tears couldn't be controlled anymore. They needed to come out. The dam wall had broken.

Gage reached for April as Saxon and Ben quickly released her from the binding restraints around her wrists. He scooped April up into his arms, pulling her onto his lap. Saxon and Ben moved in until they had surrounded their mate with their bodies. They tried to comfort her, Gage holding her against his chest, Ben at her back, and Saxon at her side. He rubbed her with his large hands, trying to comfort her, caressing her skin anywhere he could touch. The noises April made sounded like a wounded animal. He wanted to take her pain away and bear it for her himself. April cried for what seemed like hours. She tore his heart out with her pain. Her tears finally began to calm, until her body was spasming with hiccups as she lay slumped against his chest. Finally her breathing evened out, her tight muscles relaxing. She had cried herself to sleep.

Gage picked her up and stood, cradling their mate in his arms, against his chest, the occasional spasm still wracking her body. He walked into the bathing room, down the steps into the pool, and sat with her on his lap as Saxon and Ben washed and soothed April. Gage massaged her from head to foot, knowing even though he told himself he was trying to give her comfort and make sure she would feel clean when she woke, he was doing it for himself, as well. He had a need to touch his mate, to show her he loved her with his whole heart, and finally to prove that she was real. Really here, with them. Not just a figment of his imagination. Someone he would shower with love, cherish with his body until death separated them once and for all.

Chapter Ten

April woke hours later to find herself surrounded by heat. She moved her head to see Ben and Saxon lying on either side of her in bed. Gage was lying between her legs, his head resting on her stomach. She was totally naked, without any bedcovers, and knew she would never have any need for them with her mates surrounding her with their body heat. April's legs were aching from being in one position for so long. She had to move them to relieve that ache. She tried to move without disturbing her mates, but they seemed to be attuned to her, because they all sat up to look at her at the same time.

"How are you feeling, sweetheart?" Gage asked from his position between her thighs.

"Okay," April replied, heat suffusing her face as she remembered how she had cried all over him.

"You have no need to be embarrassed about feeling, honey. We love you, April, don't you get that? We want to spend the rest of our lives with you, make babies with you, grow old with you. We want you to be happy. Do you think you could be happy, here with us?" Ben asked her.

"I don't know. I'm not like you. I can't change my shape like you can. I don't think your people will ever accept me. I'm too different."

"April, you have already been accepted by our people. They would all give their lives for you. Don't you know that? You took a blade in the shoulder, which was meant for Saxon. You made me see how hard my people work and that they should have their bellies full of food before we do. They have accepted you, the way you have accepted them. You place the needs of our people before your own, which is the way it should be. You have shown me how selfish I have been, how I took my own people for granted. For that, I thank you. I love you, too, April. We have all accepted you for who you are, not what you can and can't do. You are the most loving, compassionate woman I have ever met. Please, will you stay and accept us as your mates?" Gage asked.

April didn't need to think about it anymore. Other than Olivia, she had nothing to go back home to. She was already home. "Yes. I love you, too. I love all of you. I don't know how or why I came to be here, but I never want to go back."

"Will you let us love you, honey?" Ben asked from her side. He was stroking her arm with light, delicate touches, making her flesh rise with goose bumps.

"Yes. Please, make love to me, all of you."

April looked at Ben as he leaned over her and took her mouth with his own. He was gentle at first, coaxing her to respond to him. He licked his tongue along the seam of her mouth until she opened up to him. She heard him growl deep in his throat as he ravaged her. His tongue slid in between her lips, sliding along then tangling with hers. He moved his hand down over her jaw, neck, and chest, until he held her breast in his hand. He kneaded her flesh until she cried out into his mouth, arching her chest up into his touch. She felt the mattress dip as Saxon moved closer to her, as well, and then Saxon took the turgid nipple of her other breast into his mouth.

Gage smoothed his hands up her inner thighs, pushing her legs wide apart, giving him access to her pussy. He didn't play around this time or hesitate at all. He sucked her clit into his mouth, framing it with his teeth, flicking his rough, raspy tongue over her elongated flesh rapidly. The three men had April on the verge of orgasm in moments. She arched her body up off the bed, demanding the release so close to the surface. They gave her what she wanted.

Ben released her mouth, licking and nibbling his way down her neck until he reached her chest. He sucked on her hard nipple to the point of pain. She cried out into Saxon's mouth as Saxon pinched her other nipple between his finger and thumb and devoured her mouth.

Gage released her clit from his mouth with a loud pop, and then his fingers replaced his mouth. He swirled those fingers over her sensitive clitoris then filled her aching hole with two fingers from his other hand. He pumped into her with a slow, steady pace until he had her mindless with need. She felt the walls of her pussy flutter around his fingers and knew she was close to her peak. She felt him twist his fingers around, until his hand was palm up, massaging the walls of her vagina as he moved. His digits pushed into her body as deep as possible. She arched up, begging to be touched. He pumped his fingers in and out of her pussy, curving them up as he slid against her sweet spot. He slid those two fingers in and out of her faster and faster, harder and deeper, then pulled at her labia from the top, exposing her clit to his fingers, and she knew he was releasing it from the protection of its little hood.

April pulled her mouth from Saxon's as she sobbed out loud. Her whole body was on fire, burning up from the inside out. Liquid, molten lava flowed through her, making her limbs tremble, her pussy convulse, and her breath rasp in and out of her lungs. She felt her body striving for something she'd never felt before. She was afraid to let go, afraid she would lose herself, but she knew they wouldn't let her.

"Don't fight it, baby. We just want to show you how much we love you. Let it go. You won't fall, April. We'll catch you," Saxon whispered into her ear.

April threw her head back and screamed out her release. She had never felt anything like it. It was the same as the last time they had pleasured her, but totally different. Maybe it was because they now knew she loved them and they loved her. Her pussy clamped down hard onto the fingers Gage was thrusting in and out of her body while he lapped at her clit. Thoughts vanished from her mind as pleasure consumed her whole body. She was jerking uncontrollably, her muscles spasming and twitching, her cunt expelling cum in a liquid rush. Gage didn't stop his fingers sliding in and out of her as she began to come down. No, he upped the ante. He slid the pads of his fingers over the sweet spot he'd found inside her, massaging that flesh as he pumped his fingers in and out. He sent her off again, her body beyond her control as she jerked and thrashed from the pleasure, her pussy spurting more cream from her body, covering Gage and herself with her cum. She couldn't catch her breath. Her lungs were screaming for oxygen as she panted rapidly. Finally, when she didn't think she could bear any more, her twitching body slowed, her muscles feeling like cooked noodles and her lungs finally getting the oxygen they craved.

April finally opened her eyes to see all three of her mates grinning down at her. They looked so pleased with themselves at having given her so much pleasure. April felt the corners of her mouth turn up in response to the joy and love she could see on their faces as they looked at her. She felt the grin on her face spread and knew they could see the love she had for them in her eyes, as well.

"Wow," April said around her grin. "Can we do that again?"

Her men burst out laughing. Gage and Ben traded places. Ben was now kneeling between her spread thighs. He picked her up and, without any preamble, impaled April onto his hard, throbbing cock. He leaned down and took her mouth with his own, the carnality of the kiss quickly setting fire to April once more until she was again burning from the inside out. April tried to wrestle control from her gentle bear, but he was having none of that. He grasped her hips and held her steady, all the while ravishing her mouth. April moaned out her protestations until she felt warm, wet fingers begin to massage her puckered ass. She pulled back from Ben's mouth and turned her head to see Saxon kneeling up behind her. She turned her head the other way, only to have Gage's cock brush across the lips of her mouth as she moved.

April didn't hesitate. She opened her mouth and licked around the head of Gage's cock. She groaned as she licked over the small slit at the top of his penis, tasting his pre-cum along with his flesh. It wasn't enough. She didn't think she'd ever get enough of her men. She opened her mouth wide and slowly sank down on him. The sound of Gage's moan was like music to her ears, so she moved back up his length, opened her mouth again, then slid back down. She was the one moaning as she glided back over his flesh as Saxon thrust two of his fingers into her ass, stretching her tight muscles out.

April was breathing in and out of her nose rapidly as she got into a rhythm, bobbing up and down on Gage's cock. When she felt Gage hit the back of her throat, she felt her muscles convulse as her gag reflex kicked in. Gage pulled back, but April dug her fingers into his thighs, letting him know she didn't want him to move. She repeated the process until she was able to take him down her throat. Her muscles finally obeyed her mind, relaxing at her command as she breathed in and out of her nose. She swallowed around the head of his cock to get rid of the saliva pooling in her mouth and was delighted to hear Gage yell out from the pleasure her actions gave him.

"Fuck, sweetheart. That feels so good."

April was the one moaning next, as Saxon began to push his oil-covered cock into her asshole. She tried to release her muscles as he slowly but firmly forged his way into her body. She groaned again when Saxon slid his cock back, until just the tip was still enveloped by her sphincter. She knew the vibrations from her throat were enough to tip Gage over the edge of his control. He moaned out loud and grabbed her hair in one of his hands then began to thrust his cock in and out of her mouth.

April couldn't stop the noises emitting from her throat as Saxon and Ben began to set up a slow, steady rhythm. They pumped in and out of her ass and pussy, one of them always buried in one of her holes as the other slid out. All the while, Gage pumped in and out of her mouth. She could feel the coil in her lower belly begin to tauten, her pelvic floor muscles beginning to flutter around the shafts pumping in and out of her body. Ben and Saxon picked up the pace until they were pounding in and out of her holes, fast, hard, and deep. April had to close her eyes as black spots began to dance before her vision. And then she was there. Right on the edge of that cliff, knowing she was about to fall over the edge, wanting to stop the rush of pleasure, but wanting it, needing it more. She let herself go. Let the men loving her push her up and over, making her scream as she flew apart.

April heard Gage's roar just before he pushed to the back of her throat, his semen spewing from the end of his cock as he reached his peak with her. Saxon and Ben bellowed in the next instant, and she felt her body being pumped full of their cum. Her whole body was once again shaking, and she felt her cunt push out her cum to drench Ben. Then her walls contracted back in as her muscles gripped their cocks again. She tried to open her eyes as her body quieted, slumping down onto Ben's chest, but her eyelids were too heavy for her to keep open. She felt Saxon pull then slide out of her ass and groaned when her body's reflexes took over, clamping down on him as he withdrew. That was the last thing she remembered as her tired, satiated mind and body slid down into slumber.

Chapter Eleven

April yawned and stretched, then groaned as her aching muscles protested the movement. She opened her eyes to see her mates still lying in bed with her. She didn't know exactly what time it was, but from the sunlight streaming in through the window, she knew it had to be close to midday.

Gage lifted up over her body, kissed her lips, then moved back again with a big smile on his face. "How do you feel, sweetheart?"

"Sore, but good."

"You're one hell of a woman, honey," Ben whispered then kissed her lips, as well.

"I love you, baby," Saxon stated then kissed her, too.

"Come on. Up and at 'em, lazy bones. We have things to do," Gage said as he tapped April's ass.

"Like what?" April asked then covered her mouth as she yawned.

"It's a surprise. Come on, time's wasting," Saxon replied.

"Let me have a quick wash. Oh, what am I going to wear? You guys ruined my clothes."

Gage didn't say anything. He just grabbed her hand and led her toward a closet. He opened the door and swept his hand along the feminine clothes hanging from a metal bar. She reached up and placed her hands on his shoulders, pulling him down to her, and kissed him with gratitude, then gave him a smile and wink.

"Oh, thanks. I'm glad I won't have to walk around naked," April said, then headed to the bathing chamber.

She was back in moments, clean and dry. The only problem she had was her damp hair. Since she didn't know if they had any hair dryers and really couldn't be bothered drying it, she got dressed, then braided her hair to keep it back off her face. She pulled at the soft material her men had used to tie her up with last night and turned toward Gage.

"Do you have any more of this material?"

"Yes, why do you want it?"

"I need to tie my hair up. It helps to keep me cooler with it off my neck. I thought I could tear a bit of this material to use."

Gage walked to April, took the material from her, pushed one of his claws out from the tip of his finger, and ripped the material. He took her braid from her hand and tied the material at the end of her hair.

"Thank you," April said.

"You're welcome. Come on, let's go and eat, then we will take you to your surprise," Gage commanded.

Since April was hungry, as well as thirsty, she didn't quibble over the fact he had ordered her. She let her men lead her back to the banquet dining room, where everyone was gathered for mid-sun meal.

Once they'd all eaten their fill and satisfied their thirst, Saxon helped April from her seat and led her out into the gardens. They led her to her favorite spot near the fish pond. April looked at them quizzically when she didn't notice any difference. Ben placed his hands on April's shoulders and gently turned her around to the bench. Except the bench was gone. In its place was a low-slung hammock wide enough for three or more people. Pillows were strewn along the top and bottom of the hammock, obviously placed there for comfort. April felt tears fill her eyes. No one had ever done anything for her or given her anything just because they could. She felt love for her mates fill her up with warmth and joy and knew even though she would miss Olivia terribly, she could never live without her mates at her side. April grabbed her mates and pulled them in close to her. She tried to hug them all at once, but of course, that was an impossibility. She ended up kissing and hugging them one at a time as she thanked them for their generosity.

"We didn't do this for you, April. Our people did this for you, in appreciation of the love, respect, and acceptance you have shown them and us," Saxon said.

April looked up as she heard clapping to her left. She couldn't see everyone and knew she still had a lot of names to learn, but on the smiling faces of her new family, she saw pride, love, and acceptance. By the time the clapping finally ceased, April once again had tears in her eyes. She was too choked up to speak very much, so all she said was, "Thank you."

April couldn't believe how much she had cried since she'd met her mates. She had never been one of those females who cried at the drop of a hat. Maybe because her life had been turned upside down and out of her control, then finally right side up again, she'd needed to release all the stress from the upheaval and uncertainty she had endured. She vowed not to cry anymore. She would live, laugh, and be happy instead.

As the members of the panther clan took their leave, they all bowed to their Alphas, smiled, and left the newly mated leaders alone. When everyone was gone, Saxon swooped in, swept April from her feet, and lowered her to the large hammock. April let her body relax into the molding, stretchy material hugging her body. She felt very decadent lying on the hammock as her mates looked down at her, smiling indulgently.

"I love this spot. It's the most peaceful place in the whole gardens. Your people shouldn't have done this for me. It will only encourage me to become lazy. I could spend hours out here, reading, daydreaming, and just being lazy."

"That's the whole idea, honey, and they're our people, not just Gage and Saxon's. They're ours, they belong to you, as well," Ben stated, helping April out of the hammock when she tried to rise.

April ignored his comment regarding the members of the panther clan. Instead she laughed as Ben scooped her up and out of the hammock. "I think I'll need to practice getting in and out of that thing."

"Someone will always be within calling distance, sweetheart. If you have trouble, all you have to do is ask for help," Gage replied.

"Hm," April said, not really commenting. "What happened to Vanessa?"

"She is being held in the dungeons until we decide what her punishment is to be," Saxon answered.

"I thought you'd already punished her by banishing her from the clan. What more can you do?" April asked.

"It is up to the elders and us to decide what is to become of her. We will have a trial of sorts and decide from there," Saxon replied through clenched teeth.

"What are your usual punishments?" April asked, a sinking feeling in her gut. She was afraid to hear the answer, but for her own sanity, she wanted to know.

"I don't think we should discuss this right now," Gage stated as he turned away from her.

"Please don't tell me someone will kill her. Please, you can't kill another human being. It's not right."

"Was it right when she nearly killed you? How can you not want to reciprocate in kind?" Gage asked April as he turned to face her.

"Two wrongs don't make a right. Why can't you just banish her from the pack? What gives you the right to play God? What gives you the right to decide when someone dies? Please don't, Gage. I couldn't live with myself, knowing it was my fault she was killed. I can't and won't live with that guilt on my conscience."

April heard Gage sigh, and he looked from Saxon to Ben and back again. She could see he didn't want to relent on his decision, but she knew he would now she had voiced her opinion. Their rocky relationship was too new to be put under the strain of that type of guilt, and she could see Gage was going to relent to her wishes.

"All right. See to it, Saxon. But let her know, if she comes anywhere near our land or our mate again, she will die," Gage commanded as he looked at April.

"Thank you, Gage. You won't regret it," April said and smiled with relief.

"I hope not," Gage muttered under his breath.

* * * *

The next few weeks were the best of April's life. She worked with the members of the panther clan, learning names and tasks and generally enjoying life. She felt free to be herself, not having to measure up to anyone else's expectations. Her mates spent each night loving her into oblivion, making sure she reached her own pleasure several times before they even made love to her. She was becoming more confident and carefree. She thought of Olivia often and hoped her friend was all right. She wished there was some way she could get word to her, to let her know that she was safe. But it would be even better if Olivia could come to this place and be with her.

April had just finished with Layla in the kitchen, discussing the evening meal with her and her loyal kitchen hands. She was feeling rather hot and bothered. In fact, she was feeling downright dreadful. Her skin felt clammy, her stomach was nauseous, and she was feeling rather light headed. April thought maybe the heat of the kitchen was getting to her, and she was also a little dehydrated. She grabbed a large glass of water and made her way out of the kitchen, toward the gardens outside. April was feeling decidedly shaky when she reached her hammock. She slid into the hammock and laid her head back on the pillows as she sipped at the water. The breeze on her sweaty skin helped her to feel a little better, as did the water. The nausea in her stomach began to pass, and with it, so did the trembling feeling. She finished her water, placed the glass down onto the ground, and closed her eyes. She had no idea how long she lay in the hammock dozing, but the next time she opened her eyes was to see the leering face of

Vanessa leaning over her.

April opened her mouth to call for help, but the feel of an elongated claw at her throat stopped her. She knew one swipe of that claw would be enough to kill her. She lay there staring at the crazed woman, not daring to move or make a sound.

"You should have let them kill me, you stupid bitch. They are going to want me back once I take care of you. They won't want to leave me again. They will ask me back into their beds with open arms once you're dead."

"I feel really sorry for you, Vanessa. Especially if you believe that rubbish you're spouting. Those three men love me and will never ask you back into their bed. They are my mates, and I am theirs. You won't live five minutes when they find out you've killed me," April stated.

"That's what you think, you stupid human. They've been coming to my bed in the dungeons every night, spending themselves in my body, pumping me full of their seed. They want me to have their babies. Babies that will be able to change form and not be a half-breed human," Vanessa spat.

"You're delusional, Vanessa. Those three men have spent every minute of every night in my bed. I don't know who you've been fucking, but it definitely wasn't my mates."

Vanessa's scream of rage echoed throughout the gardens, alerting the seasoned warriors nearby to her presence. April watched as the woman's face began to contort, fur springing up all over her skin, her body shifting, her bones cracking and popping, conforming to her new shape. April watched as Vanessa backed up slowly on her four paws and hunkered down, ready to pounce on her and rip her throat out. April didn't move. She knew she didn't stand a chance against the crazy panther woman, so she closed her eyes and waited for her own death.

April's eyes snapped open when she heard a thud and loud growls. She was surrounded by large black panthers, their muscles tense as they waited to protect their Alpha female. Only one panther was fighting the smaller, female panther, and April knew Vanessa didn't stand a chance. She closed her eyes and tried to block out the sounds of the fight between the two large cats. The sounds were terrifying and vicious, but April knew Vanessa only had herself to blame. The noise was gone, and not a sound could be heard. No birds chirped, no small animals rustling beneath leaves, foraging for food. Only the harsh sound of her own breathing. Vanessa was dead. Cedric, the lead warrior, second in command to her mates, had killed her.

Chapter Twelve

Gage needed to take a run in his beast form and knew his friend and brother were suffering the same urges. He, Saxon, and Ben kissed their mate good-bye, with the promise to be back in a couple of hours. His mate was becoming more demanding as her belly swelled with their child. None of them knew which of them was the father, but to him, it didn't matter. Any child April had would be loved and cared for. As far as he was concerned, they were all the fathers, regardless of whose sperm had actually joined with their mate's egg. He didn't mind her demanding them to make love to her throughout the hours of the day. In fact, he was thankful there were three of them so they could each take a turn at keeping their mate satisfied. He had no idea if their mate's sex drive was because of her pregnancy or just the plain fact she loved her mates and couldn't keep her hands off of them. Not that he was complaining. He loved it that their mate was so insatiable, needing them to touch her and love her all the time, but their beasts were feeling a little restless and they needed to let them free for a couple of hours.

Gage and his brother changed and took off, leaving Ben to lumber behind them. His and his brother's panthers were a lot faster than Ben's bear, so he and Saxon found themselves in the forest near the tree where they had first found their mate. Gage and his brother waited languorously on the large branches as they waited for Ben to catch up. Ben was just lumbering up the track toward him when Gage saw the air around him shimmer. He saw Ben freeze in his tracks as he sniffed the air. Gage and his brother sniffed the strange scent on their air, as well. The scent they caught on the breeze was familiar yet different. Gage kept still when he heard footsteps heading their way.

* * * *

April had felt the need to follow her mates into the forest. She didn't usually, but today, for some reason, she just knew she had to be near them. She knew she was probably going to get into trouble from her men, especially her demandingly arrogant Gage, but she wasn't worried. She only ended up feeling pleasure when he, Saxon, and Ben punished her. She wasn't silly, though. She had found Cedric and asked him to come along with her so she would be safe as she walked along the forest trail. Of course, since Cedric was second in command to her mates and in charge of the warriors, he had decided to bring along his brother Hugh and five other warriors. She thought that was just a tad paranoid, but she hadn't argued with him.

April was glad when she spotted Ben up ahead. She was feeling so big and cumbersome. Her belly was bulging and heavy in front of her. She couldn't wait for labor to begin so she could hold her baby in her arms and get her body back to normal. She waddled quickly until she was at Ben's side. She saw his eyes widen at her then narrow as he glared.

"Ben, where are Gage and Saxon? Don't look at me like that. I'm not stupid. Cedric and the others are behind me. I just had this urge to come and look for you. I thought you needed me," April said then wrapped her arms around the bear's neck, giving him a hug.

"A–April, is that you? Are you out of your mind, girlfriend? Get away from that bear before he eats you for dinner."

"Olivia? Oh my God. Olivia. How did you get here? Are you all right? You look like you've seen a ghost," April stated as she hurried as much as she could toward her friend and hugged her. "You have no idea how much I've missed you."

"Are you crazy? There's a large bear behind you and you look like you're going for a stroll in the park. Come on, we have to get out of here," Olivia said as she grabbed April's wrist, trying to tug her along with her.

"Oh, he won't hurt you. He's my mate, and those two up there are my mates, as well," April stated cheerfully, pointing up into the branches above Olivia's head.

April watched her friend look up into the tree to see Gage and Saxon lying on a tree limb above her, in their panther form. She saw her friend's eyes widen as she turned back to her. April heard the warriors walking up behind her and felt Ben nudge her lightly on her thigh with his nose. She watched Olivia back away from her as Ben began to change from his bear form. Olivia's face paled when Ben's bones cracked and popped as they contorted until her man was once again standing at her side, totally naked. Then she frowned with concern when she saw Olivia's eyes roll back in her head as she swayed on her feet. April knew she wouldn't reach Olivia before her friend hit the ground.

April heard movement behind her and then she saw Cedric rushing toward Olivia. He caught her friend before she hit the ground, scooping her up into his arms. She watched as Cedric leaned down and sniffed at the skin on Olivia's neck. Cedric looked up at her and Ben and then he glared at the other warriors behind her. His eyes were changing from their usual color to gold and back again, as he turned toward his brother. Hugh rushed over to Olivia and Cedric, and April saw him lean down to sniff at her friend, as well. The two brothers roared loud and long with passion and possessiveness.

April gasped with wonder when she heard two words uttered from Cedric with guttural covetousness. "Mine. Mate."

April was too astounded to react at first. It took a moment or two for Cedric's words to sink in. When they did, she threw her head back and laughed.

What more could a woman ask for? She had three wonderful mates whom she loved more than anything, and they returned that love. She was about to have a baby, and now her best friend was by her side, once more. Life just didn't get any better than that!

THE END

WWW.BECCAVAN-EROTICROMANCE.COM

ABOUT THE AUTHOR

My name is Becca Van. I live in Australia with my wonderful hubby of many years, as well as my children, a pigeon pair, (a girl and a boy). I have always wanted to write and last year decided to do just that.

I didn't want to stay in the mainstream of a boring nine-to-five job, so I quit, fulfilling my passion for writing. I decided to utilize my time with something I knew I would enjoy and had always wanted to do. I submitted my first manuscript to Siren-BookStrand a couple of months ago, and much to my excited delight, I got a reply saying they would love to publish my story. I literally jump out of bed with excitement each day and can't wait for my laptop to power up so I can get to work.

Also by Becca Van

Ménage Everlasting: Terra-form 2: *Taming Olivia*
Ménage Everlasting: Terra-form 3: *Keeley's Opposition*

For all other titles, please visit
www.bookstrand.com/becca-van

Siren Publishing, Inc.
www.SirenPublishing.com

CPSIA information can be obtained at www.ICGtesting.com
Printed in the USA
LVOW04s1703140615

442438LV00022B/848/P